THE CHESTER COUNTY BOYS

Marlene Mitchell

BEARHEAD PUBLISHING
- BhP -
Louisville, Kentucky

THE CHESTER COUNTY BOYS

BEARHEAD PUBLISHING
- BhP -
Louisville, Kentucky
www.bearheadpublishing.com/marlene.html

THE CHESTER COUNTY BOYS
by Marlene Mitchell

Copyright © 2006 Marlene Mitchell
ALL RIGHTS RESERVED

Cover Design by Bearhead Publishing
Cover Concept and Original Artwork by Marlene Mitchell

First Printing - September 2006

ISBN: 0-9776260-3-2
1 2 3 4 5 6 7 8 9

NO PART OF THIS BOOK MAY BE REPRODUCED IN ANY FORM, BY PHOTOCOPYING OR BY ANY ELECTRONIC OR MECHANICAL MEANS, INCLUDING INFORMATION STORAGE OR RETRIEVAL SYSTEMS, WITHOUT PERMISSION IN WRITING FROM THE COPYRIGHT OWNER / AUTHOR.

Disclaimer

This book is a work of fiction. The characters, names, places, and incidents are used fictitiously and are a product of the author's imagination. Any resemblance of actual persons, living or dead, is entirely coincidental.

.Proudly printed in the United States of America.

Dedication

To my friend, Janet Dial, who left this earth too soon. I miss her. She will always be in my memories.

To Norma
Best Wishes
Pauline Mitchell

Other Novels by Marlene Mitchell

Yard Sale - Everything Must Go

Return to Ternberry

CHAPTER ONE

Carly put two quarters into the soda machine and waited for the familiar sound of the can falling into the dispenser. The machine grumbled for a moment, then went silent. Carly hit the machine with the back of her hand and jiggled the coin return.

"Come on," Danny yelled as he opened the car door. "I've just put another gallon of water in the radiator. I want to get going before it starts leaking again."

"I need a soda. The machine ate my money," Carly replied, jiggling the coin return again.

Danny slammed the car door and hopped onto the wooden porch of the store. "Watch out!" He raised his foot and with the heel of his boot kicked the machine sending two sodas clamoring into Carly's hands. "There's your damn soda. Now let's go."

The heat formed a mirage of waves on the open road. At times the dust was so thick Carly had to roll up the window to keep from choking. She hated these trips to Lawton and promised herself this would be the last. There was no reason for her to come. Danny's parents did not like her any more than she liked them, yet he insisted she make the trip with him. Carly wiped the dust from her eyes and rolled a soda can across her forehead. "What did you get your dad for this birthday?"

The Chester County Boys

"Same thing I get him every year; a six pack and a carton of cigarettes. The old man would be disappointed if I got him anything else. Damn, it's hot in here. Roll down the window," Danny grumbled.

Carly slowly rolled down the window and tasted the Texas dust. She didn't want to argue with Danny any more today. She laid her head back on the seat and closed her eyes.

Danny had started off the morning cursing because there was no milk for his cereal. He sent the bowl crashing to the floor. She pretended to have a headache and wanted to stay home. He cursed at her and slammed the bathroom door so hard, the mirror fell off the wall. When she put on a pair of cutoffs and a tee shirt, he made her change into jeans, even though it was almost a hundred degrees outside. All they did was argue and she was tired of it. She sucked in her breath, wishing she had enough nerve to tell him right now that she was leaving him. Her head jolted forward as Danny tried to swerve around an old pickup truck in front of him.

"You stupid yahoo, get off the road!" Danny yelled, his middle finger protruding out the window. He slammed his hand down on the horn, his car almost touching the bumper of the truck. Carly dug her nails into the seat of the car. She knew better than to say anything to him about his driving.

Danny fidgeted, his head darting in and out of the car window. "I can't believe this. This ass is driving twenty miles an hour and he won't let me pass." Danny picked up a full soda can off of the front seat and hurled it out of the window. The can exploded on the roof of the truck. The truck swerved to the right, giving Danny just enough room to pass. Carly could see the look of fear on the old man's face as they passed the truck. She mouthed the words, "I'm sorry."

Marlene Mitchell

Steam began to escape from under the hood by the time they reached Lawton. Danny coasted the last half-mile to his parent's house and let the car roll to a stop at the end of the driveway. His mother opened the door, wiping her hands on her apron. "It's about time. I thought you weren't coming. Why did you park way down there?" she yelled.

"I told you we were coming, didn't I? Where's Ed? I need to talk to him about a car."

"Well, hello to you, too," Shirley whined.

Danny passed his mother and headed toward the kitchen.

"Damn, it's hotter than hell in here. How come you don't have the air-conditioner on?"

"Cause, I'm cooking, that's why. Those window units can't keep this place cool. Your father has the one in the living room turned down so low my bill is going to be sky high. Ed ain't here, he's working today. Go say happy birthday to your dad. He's in the living room." Shirley turned to see Carly still standing in the doorway, holding the beer and carton of cigarettes. "Oh, it's you. Well, close the door before you let the flies in."

Danny's father, Marvin, reclined in his leather lounge chair wearing a tee shirt, boxer shorts and his boots. The room was frigid as the cold air poured out of the air conditioner. He reached for the cigarettes and nodded to Carly. Marvin never had much to say. He spent most of his time just trying to stay out of Shirley's way and watching his sixty-four inch television. Shirley had allowed him that one luxury after his retirement from the auto factory. Danny popped the top on two beers and handed one to his dad. He plopped down on the sofa. Carly shivered and went back into the kitchen. "Is there anything I can

The Chester County Boys

help you with?" she asked as Shirley rolled out biscuits onto the kitchen table.

"No, but you could go outside and tell Erlene to turn off the hose. Those boys have been playing in that water for over an hour. I swear my water bill is going to be out of sight this month."

Erlene Reedy sat in a lawn chair painting her nails while her two boys ran back and forth through the water screaming and pushing each other. Erlene grabbed the hose out of her son's hand as he ran by. She turned when the back door opened. "Oh, hi, Carly, I didn't hear you guys pull in. You boys stop hollering and go get dressed, right now." She stomped her foot and pointed toward the door. The boys ignored her and ran off screaming into the yard. Erlene laid the hose down and let the water run over her feet.

Carly sat in the chair next to her and took off her shoes. "I don't know whether to go in the living room and freeze or sit out here and burn up."

"I know. It's a real scorcher and Ed had to work today. I knew he would saddle me with coming up here to see his parents. He knows his momma doesn't like me and I sure could go a long time without seeing her ugly face." Erlene jumped up and yelled at the boys. "I'm telling you for the last time, turn off the water and go inside and get dressed! "How is everything going with you and Danny? Any bruises yet?"

Carly did not answer her. From the first time they met, Erlene always made a point of telling Carly the same stories about Danny over and over. It was as if she couldn't wait to prove to Carly that Danny was a real hot head. Erlene told her about the time in high school when Danny's girlfriend, Kim, broke up with him. He hit her and then took a baseball bat to

Kim's father's car. Erlene said that Danny's first wife had more black eyes than a prizefighter.

Today her questions made Carly feel uneasy. Danny had abused her several times in the past month. Once when she told him she was leaving, his hand closed around her throat and his fingers pressed into her neck until she began to cry. Although he had apologized later, she still wondered how much he was capable of. Even worse, an insatiable appetite for sex always followed his fits of anger. It seemed like hurting her gave him sexual excitement. Erlene's whiny voice interrupted her thoughts.

"I'm going to leave Ed in about another year," Erlene said in a matter of fact voice, as she wiped the droplets of perspiration from her forehead. "I've been cutting a little money out of the household expenses each week and in about another year I'll be able to leave him and find me a new place to live on my own." She laughed. "Sometimes when Ed comes home really drunk, I take money out of his wallet. He never says a word. Probably figured he just spent it on some bimbo in the bar. Yeah, Ed thinks I'm real stupid, but I know what he's doing and he's gonna be sorry when I take off. I ain't that bad looking. I can get someone else." She ran her hand over the front of the skimpy sundress covering the breasts that Ed had bought her for their tenth anniversary.

"How can you just sit here and say that so calmly? What about the boys?" Carly asked.

"Hey it's Ed's turn to deal with these hellions. I've been taking care of them for the last ten years. Did he think it was easy taking care of the twins while he was out running around? Besides, he's got those boys so rotten that they don't mind me anyway. He tells them that they don't have to do what I say and

The Chester County Boys

he buys them anything they want. Now don't you say anything to Danny about what I just told you because he'll run right to his big brother and tell him everything. You ought to get smart and make a run for it too. You know these Reedy boys aren't easy to get away from."

Shirley opened the back door and yelled. "You two gonna sit out there all day and talk? Erlene, you get those boys away from my gnomes. They're gonna break them. It's almost time to eat." Erlene made a face. "I hate that old bat. She's got more concrete statues in this yard than a cemetery. Maybe she can take care of Ed when I'm gone. They deserve each other. Come on we better go in before she gets real mad."

Carly knew that before dinner was over Shirley would bring up the subject of marriage. It only took her a few minutes for her to ask the same question.

"So, you two any closer to getting married or are you still gonna continue living in sin?" she said staring at Carly.

"Look, it's our business if we decide to get married. Now you tell me why you had to cook a roast when it's a hundred degrees in here?" Danny growled.

"Can you all let me just enjoy my meal in peace?" Marvin asked as he shoveled potatoes into his mouth.

Danny stuck his knife into a large hunk of meat. "I'm thinking we may get married when the weather gets cooler. Maybe in September." He stuffed the meat into his mouth.

"Oh, that would be just wonderful," Shirley purred. "Why we could have the wedding here. I could decorate the backyard and it would be real nice. Erlene can help me make potato salad and your daddy could grill the meat."

Carly looked up in surprise. They had never talked about marriage. The thought made her feel queasy inside. Shirley was interrupted by one of the twins.

"I can't eat this crap," he whined. "I want to go to McDonalds."

"Curtis Lee, just shut your mouth and eat. Grandma has cake." Erlene gave Shirley a limp smile. Both of the boys got up from the table.

Carly stared at her plate ignoring the ridiculous conversation. Pushing the greasy meat to the side, she tried to eat a couple of bites of the lumpy potatoes. She knew that Shirley was watching her, but this time she wasn't going to pretend that she could eat her disgusting food. She picked up her plate and headed toward the kitchen.

"Now, where you going? You didn't finish your food either. You sick or something?" Shirley asked in her usual irritable voice.

"No, I'm just not very hungry." She left the room under the glaring eyes of Danny and his mother.

"You're gonna miss cake," Shirley yelled after her.

After dinner, Danny joined Carly on the porch. He leaned his chair against the wall and lit a cigarette. "How come you're never nice to my mom? She knows you don't like her. I don't think it would hurt if every once in a while you would say something nice to her. We gotta talk about this car situation. How much money you got, Carly?" he asked, as he opened his wallet and pulled out a few bills. "I got about forty dollars on me. I just talked to Ed and he said if we come down to the car lot, he'll give me a real good deal and we can leave your old junker here as a trade-in."

Carly reached into her back pocket and pulled out her money. "I only have twenty dollars. I didn't know you were planning on buying a car today."

Danny screwed up his face and mimicked her in a whining voice. "I didn't know you were going to buy a car today. Well, we sure can't make it home in that hunk of crap and there ain't no use putting another dime in it to make it run cause it would still be crap. Maybe we can take a cab," Danny said, sarcastically. He shoved the chair back and got up. "I'm going to drink a beer with my dad; then you and me are going down to the car lot. Go help my mother with the dishes."

Carly cringed at the thought of being even close to Danny's older brother, Ed Reedy. He always managed to put his hands somewhere on her body where they didn't belong and make some vulgar remark. Even though Erlene wasn't one of her favorite people, Carly felt sorry for her having to live in the same house with such a slime like Ed.

CHAPTER TWO

Ed's Used Car Lot was in the center of downtown Lawton. Ed called his lot one fine piece of real estate. He had taken the business over when his father-in-law retired. Although he made quite a bit of money, he liked to squander it on gambling and women. His crackpot staff of mechanics were able to make even the biggest hunk of junk purr like a kitten, at least until the car was about a mile from the lot. Ed's cars came with no guarantees. He said that's why he could give his customers such good deals. People with bad credit and very little money were his favorite customers. They were at his mercy.

    Ed stood on the small porch of the trailer he used for his office, smoking a cigar. As soon as Carly got out of the car, he grinned and put his arm around her. "How are you, you sweet thing? Long time no see and how's my little brother?" Carly tried to pull away as his hand traveled down her side. "Now you be nice to me and maybe I can find something on this lot that can make us both happy." He squeezed her arm, pushing his hand into her breast.

    Carly struggled away from him and opened the door to the trailer. "I'll wait inside for you, Danny."

    Carly watched from the small trailer window as one of the mechanics pulled a maroon Thunderbird to the front of the

The Chester County Boys

lot. Danny walked around the car with Ed right behind him. She watched as Ed opened the hood and pointed to the engine. A few minutes later they entered the office. Carly pushed a chair close to the wall and sat down. Ed threw his hat on the desk. "That's a purring son of a bitch, Danny. You know damn well I wouldn't sell you a lemon. I was thinking about keeping that car for myself, but I'm glad you're the one buying it. I always save the best cars for my favorite people. Now how are you going to pay for this baby? I'm gonna give it to you for a grand."

"I guess I'll have to finance it, Ed. I'm low on funds right now," Danny said.

"You got any collateral? I know your credit isn't any good." Ed sat on the edge of the desk staring at Carly. "Maybe I could take it out in trade," he said patting Carly on the knee. He let out a bellow of laughter, revealing his tobacco-stained teeth.

Carly jumped up and threw her credit card on the desk. "You are such a bastard, Ed Reedy! Here, put the charges on this and put the damn car in my name." She folded her arms across her chest, and waited for Ed to get over the shock of her outburst.

"Well, that's the thanks I get for trying to help out family. You know I just love to joke with you and watch your pretty little face turn red," Ed said as he ran her credit card through the machine. "I'll send you the papers in the mail."

"That's fine and by the way, I'm not family." Carly grabbed the keys and card off the desk and slammed the trailer door.

They argued all the way home to Sweetwater. Danny was furious at the way Carly had talked to Ed and that she refused to go back to his mother's house for coffee and birthday cake. "And another thing, Carly," Danny whined, "I'm tired of you not doing what I say. I told you before to stop asking everyone you meet about that man your looking for. You even asked that guy at the service station if he knew a man named Shine. It's getting embarrassing. I told you before that this guy is either dead or just exists in your head. I thought we agreed that was part of your past and there's no sense bringing it up all the time. Now put it to rest."

"I'm not going to do it. He's out there somewhere and I'm going to find him," Carly said softly.

Without notice, he reached across the seat and slapped her. The force of the blow banged her head against the window. "You shut your mouth and don't talk back to me."

Carly slumped down in the seat, her cheek stinging from the imprint of his hand. As usual, he apologized to her, but it landed on deaf ears. Danny knew that she had been looking for Shine since she came to Texas and even agreed to help her when they first got together. Shine was her only link to her childhood. Now it was a real source of contention between her and Danny. The car engine developed a knock about thirty miles from Sweetwater and Danny cursed and banged on the steering wheel as if that would make the problem go away. He ranted that he should have never trusted Ed to sell him a good car and swore that he wouldn't pay for it, forgetting that the car was now in Carly's name and the charge was on her credit card.

It was after midnight when they arrived at the apartment. She wanted to tell him that she was leaving, but she knew that saying anything right now would throw him into a rage. After a futile attempt to avoid his advances, Carly finally gave in and stared at the water-stained ceiling as Danny's weight lay on her. A few minutes later, he groaned and rolled over. "I'm sorry I hit you again, babe, but you just got to stay in line. And next time we do it, I want you to participate. I don't like doing it with a dummy."

When he began snoring, Carly crept out of bed and into the bathroom. With the hot water running in the shower, she laid her head on the wall and cried. She didn't hear him come in. Once again he groped at her body. She could feel herself screaming inside.

CHAPTER THREE

    The breakfast crowd had already filled the truck stop restaurant when Carly arrived at work the next morning. Putting on her apron, she headed toward the kitchen. She jumped when grease spattered from the grill hitting her arm. Trying to avoid the glare from her manager, Harold, she picked up a tray of water glasses and headed toward her station. He was a sniveling little man that seemed to delight in making all of the waitresses as miserable as possible. At home, his wife was the boss. Carly knew she was late again and Harold was waiting for that moment when he could chastise her in front of the other employees. Finally cornering her behind the counter, Harold asked her in a loud voice why she was late. Carly tried to explain that her car wouldn't start and she had to take a bus. Harold never liked excuses, so there was no reason to defend herself when he went into his tirade about the need for promptness. She stood with her hands folded across her chest and listened to his tired speech with deaf ears.

    By eleven, the breakfast crowd had thinned and she busied herself cleaning up the tables and sweeping the floor. She jumped as he came up behind her and started ranting again. He hadn't got much of a reaction out of her the first time. "You were late three times this week," Harold snarled, standing inches away from Carly. "What makes you think you can come

The Chester County Boys

and go whenever you please? And I don't like you coming in here with your face all swollen. It gives the place a bad name. I've got a mind to fire you right now."

Taking off her apron, Carly handed him the broom. "Harold, you are a dumb ass. Here, you take this broom and stick it where the sun don't shine. I quit." She received a round of applause from the other waitresses behind the counter, as Harold stood with his mouth open, holding the broom.

Danny was still sleeping when she got home to the tiny apartment. She could smell the stale cigarette smoke and odor of beer still clinging to his clothes hanging on the back of the chair. He must have gone to the pool hall as soon as she left for work. He almost always drank beer for breakfast. She changed out of her uniform into jeans and a tee shirt. She quietly began doing the dishes that were left in the sink from the day before.

Tears welled up in her eyes as she watched a cockroach skitter across the counter and disappear behind the torn wallpaper. Danny had promised her that they would move as soon as he got steady work. He had been working as a bartender for over six months, but he still claimed they didn't have enough money to move. He spent most of his money on beer and drugs, leaving her to pay the bills and buy the groceries. Carly slammed the greasy frying pan on the counter, as she tried to squash another cockroach. Danny sat up in bed rubbing his eyes. "What time is it? What are you doing home?"

"It's only noon. I quit my job."

"What in the hell did you do that for? You made good money at the truck stop. Now what are we going to do?"

She whirled around, her hands clenching the sink. "Yeah, Danny, what are we going to do? I could get another job in some restaurant tomorrow and we still would be in the same situation six months from now. I'm tired of living like this. Tired of this nasty place, tired of you always stoned or drunk and tired of the way you slap me around. I think it's time we call it quits." She wasn't afraid of him this time. The anger seething inside of her was making her stronger even though she knew he would probably hit her and she was right. Danny came across the floor before she could put her arms up to protect herself. He hit her across the face, sending her reeling into the side of the refrigerator. She slid to the floor holding her nose as the blood ran down her chin.

"I'm telling you for the last time, Carly, and you better listen to me good. I love you and you aren't going anywhere. Now get that through your thick skull." He leaned down and picked her up off of the floor. Danny put his arms around her and wiped her nose with the dishtowel. "You better put some ice on that." His hand slid beneath her shirt as he pushed against her.

"No, Danny, please not now, I'm hurt," Carly said in a soft voice, trying not to provoke him any further. "Let me clean up a little. You go lay down and I'll get you a beer."

Carly looked at her reflection in the bathroom mirror. Her eye was almost swollen shut and a small cut ran across her cheek. She dabbed at her nose, wiggling it back and forth to make sure it wasn't broken. She moaned in pain as she filled the tub and sank down into the warm water trying to clear her head and decide what to do next.

"You okay in there, babe?" Danny yelled. "I'm waiting for you and my beer."

"Yeah, be right there," she said. She shifted her weight in the warm water, trying to get comfortable. She could feel a

The Chester County Boys

sore spot on her hip, where she hit the wall. By the time she emerged from the bathroom, he was asleep.

That evening when Danny left for work, she pretended to be asleep in the chair. He touched her leg, but she didn't move. She waited until after eight before she began packing her things into a canvas bag. She knew he might come back to check on her or at least call to make sure she was still there. He had done that in the past after one of their arguments. Carly decided to travel light and only take what she could carry in one bag. She had no idea where she was going, but it would be as far away from Danny Reedy as possible.

Carly ran the two blocks to the bus stop and stood in the shadows of a storefront until the bus pulled up. She rode to the end of the line and then walked another three blocks to the truck-stop restaurant. She shielded her eyes as she peered inside to make sure Harold was not there. Walking quickly to the restroom, Carly put her duffel bag in her old locker and then went outside and waited in front of the building until she saw a familiar blue and white eighteen-wheeler pull into the parking lot. She stepped into the light just as the driver slammed the door. "Hi, Rock, how you doing?" she said to the burly man, his arms covered in tattoos.

The driver squinted for a moment, shielding his eyes. "Oh, hi, Carly, I didn't recognize you without your uniform on. What are you doing here this time of night?"

"I quit my job today and I'm leaving town. I really could use a ride. Where you headed, Rock?"

"Hey that's too bad, you quitting your job and all. I'm gonna miss your good service. I'm on my way to Lubbock. You can tag along, but after I fill her up, I got to get myself something to eat. What in the world happened to your face?"

"I fell," she answered.

After Carly retrieved her bag, she climbed into the back compartment of the truck. "I'll just wait in here for you, Rock. You go get yourself something to eat." She let out a sigh of relief. Maybe this time she could get out of Sweetwater before Danny got home. He would be furious. He would probably destroy the apartment and then go on a binge. Hopefully, she would be far, far away before he decided to come looking for her.

Twenty minutes later, Rock opened the door of the truck and hopped up on the seat. A toothpick still hung from the corner of his mouth. "Are you ready to hit the road, gal?"

"I sure am," she replied.

"You want to sit up here by me?" Rock asked.

"If you don't mind I think I'll just sit back here and take a nap." Carly slipped down in the seat and closed her eyes. She listened to the hiss of the airbrakes as Rock pulled the semi on to the highway. The drone of the voices on the cb radio lulled her into a light sleep. Each turn of the wheels was taking her further away from Danny Reedy.

"He hit you again, didn't he?" Rock asked.

"Yeah," she answered quietly.

"You want me to kick his ass when I get back from Lubbock?"

"No, someday he'll get what's coming to him."

CHAPTER FOUR

Carly shielded her eyes and peered into the window of the Double L Roadhouse. The man behind the bar drying glasses shook his head and mouthed the words, "We're closed." She pointed to the "help wanted" sign. He pushed a buzzer that unlocked the door and motioned for her to come in.

"You looking for a job?" he asked

"Yes, I am," Carly replied.

"How old are you?"

"I'm twenty-four."

"I didn't see a car pull up. Are you on foot?"

Carly shook her head. "Yeah, I am. I'm going to be staying at the motel across the road for awhile. My car broke down."

He came out from behind the bar. "Wait here and I'll go get the owner. Lee is in the office."

Carly sat on a barstool waiting. When she heard the door to the office close she turned. Lee Lewis was an imposing figure, over six feet tall, with cropped black hair and a voluminous body stuffed into a denim shirt and jeans. "J.B. tells me you're looking for work."

"Yes, sir, I am."

Lee grinned. "Well just to put things straight, it's yes ma'am."

A look of surprise came over Carly's face. "Oh, my gosh, I'm sorry, I just thought..."

Lee interrupted her. "No problem. Lots of people think the same thing. Doesn't hurt my feelings one bit. Now what's going on with you? Are you running from the law?"

Carly shook her head. "No, it's nothing like that. I just needed a change of scenery."

"And you chose Lubbock? Who you trying to get away from, your husband or boyfriend?" Lee asked, pointing to the large bruise on the side of Carly's face.

"It's my ex-boyfriend."

"Look, I don't want any crazed maniac coming here and shooting up the place. Is the relationship over for good?"

"You bet. He has no idea where I am and I'd like to keep it that way."

"What about experience, you ever worked in a bar before?"

"No, but I've been a waitress most of my life."

"Well, honey, let me tell you working in a diner is nothing like working in a bar," Lee said, as she lit a cigarette. "I pay twenty bucks a night. You keep all your tips. First time I catch you stealing or skimming, you're out of here. You pay for every glass you break and you stay in your own area. You can come in tonight at eight if you want the job. It might help your tips if you have a tighter shirt than the one you have on." Lee got up and started back toward her office. "I'll leave some paper work for you to fill out. By the way, what's your name?"

"It's Carly, Carly Boone."

Carly returned to the Double L at exactly eight o'clock and waited for Lee. She had knocked on her office door, but Lee yelled at her to go wait in the bar. The bar was already crowded and three waitresses were circling among the tables.

The Chester County Boys

One by one, as they came to the side counter to fill their drink orders, they introduced themselves. Lee sauntered toward Carly. She went behind the bar and popped open a beer. "Sorry to be so cranky, Carly, but I just woke up. I was catching a little shut-eye." Lee yawned and motioned for Carly to follow her.

She showed her how to enter her tabs into the cash register and then checked to see how many bottles of beer Carly could carry at one time. Satisfied with her performance, Lee led her across the dance floor to the small bandstand. "We got a house band that's been playing here forever. They bring in a pretty good crowd. They're an odd bunch, but they know their business. They get free drinks, but only two a piece for the night. Don't let them tell you any different. Come on, I'll introduce you to them. They call themselves the Chester County Boys."

Lee pushed her way through the crowd and waved Carly to follow her up on the stage. "Guys, this is Carly. Take it easy on her. It's her first night." Lee pointed to a tall man sitting on a stool. "That one there that looks like a hound dog is Merle Hurley and right behind him is his brother, Cletus," Lee said, pointing to a small man with slicked back hair and Elvis sideburns. Merle nodded and Carly smiled. Merle really did look like an old hound dog with his sad eyes and sagging jowls.

"Jack must be over by the bar," Lee said looking around. "Jack plays the keyboard. He doesn't talk to anyone unless he has to, so don't worry if he gives you the silent treatment. Randy is the youngest. He's the drummer. Randy thinks he is a real ladies' man, so watch his hands."

A large hulking man started up the stairs to the stage. His long arms hung at his side as he lumbered along with his head down. He sat down and picked up his fiddle, never once looking up. "That's Quaid Perkins," Lee said. "I could introduce you to him, but he won't remember your name. He's peculiar, if you know what I mean. So that's the five of them and that's all you need to know. I see you already met some of the other girls. Most of them are okay. I don't keep troublemakers around here very long. So, you work hard, do a good job and you and me will get along just fine. I'm gonna set you up with a station. If you have any trouble during the night you just motion to J.B. and he'll know what to do."

Carly hesitated for a moment, "Lee, I was wondering if I could ask you a question?"

"Sure, kiddo, go ahead," Lee replied.

"I was wondering if you ever heard of a guitar player named Shine? He played with a small band and they used to travel all around Texas."

"Who, Shine? What's his last name?"

"I don't know. That's what I called him, but I thought maybe he had mentioned it to someone else along the way."

"Well, I can ask the band and J.B. Maybe they know him." Lee thought to herself. Here's another one with baggage.

After just a few minutes of training, Carly filled her first tray with bottles of cold beer and headed toward the area Lee had assigned for her. As she walked passed the stage, Cletus put on a large white hat. His red-studded shirt and pants looked out of place in front of the background of blue denim shirts and Levi's worn by the rest of the band. He strummed a chord on his guitar. Cletus bent down and winked at Carly. "Just keep the cold beer coming little lady and we'll get along just fine."

Cletus stepped up to the microphone. "Ya'll ready for some good music?"

The Chester County Boys

Randy ran across the floor and jumped onto the platform. The band broke into their first number and the floor filled with dancers. There wasn't anything unusual about the band. They played the same standard songs that Carly had heard over and over; the mechanical sets of music that they could probably play in their sleep. Cletus was the only one that seemed to be enjoying what he was doing. He would occasionally joke with someone on the dance floor as he belted out his songs in a twangy voice.

It didn't take Carly long to catch on to the routine. She learned to carry her tray high enough so that she didn't hit anyone in the head. She also caught on quickly how important it was to collect your money after each round of drinks. Her first table left without paying for two rounds of drinks. Lee totaled up the tab and told her it would be deducted from her check at the end of the week.

It was near the end of the evening on the first night. Carly's feet were aching and her arm was numb from carrying the heavy tray. She couldn't wait for her shift to be over. When the band took their last break, Randy rambled over to the bar and ordered a beer. He turned around and leaned against the brass rail. He could see Carly moving around through the dwindling crowd in her station. She wasn't really his type. She was thin, but she had a nice butt and he liked her hair. He waited until she returned to the service bar to fill her tray. "So, what's your story, Carly?" he asked.

"Just trying to do my job," she said as she put the empty glasses in the sink.

"Listen, I was wondering if you would like to go out after work and get something to eat?" He ran his hand down her arm.

Carly pushed him away. "I'm tired and when I leave here, I plan on going straight to bed," Carly replied in an irritated tone.

Randy grinned. "Hey, that sounds good to me."

"Listen to me, Randy, you keep your hands and smart remarks to yourself and we'll get along just fine. I'm not one of your bar bimbos."

Randy put his hands up. "Okay, okay. I'm sorry, but you can't blame a guy for trying."

Carly picked up her full tray. "Yes, I can, but I accept your apology."

Each night after her shift, Carly would go to her motel room and fall into a restless sleep, staying in bed most of the day. Her arms ached and she had bruises on her feet from being constantly stepped on as she moved through the crowds in the bar. The money was good once she learned to control the number of broken glasses and manage to smile once in a while.

The band drew a heavy drinking crowd on the weekends that were loose with their money, sometimes leaving her large tips. Occasionally, before she could retrieve it, a wife or girlfriend would return to the table replacing the ten for a one-dollar bill. She understood. Drinking money flowed easy.

It was her second weekend at the Double L when things began to unravel for Carly. The crowd was particularly rowdy.

J.B. had to break up two or three fights with the help of the baseball bat he kept behind the bar.

As the evening wore on, Carly's nerves were frazzled from fending off the drunks who would touch her or pull her down on their laps. One insistent customer became angry when she refused his attention and grabbed her by the arm. As she

The Chester County Boys

pulled away from him, she lost her balance and fell to the floor along with her tray filled with full bottles of beer.

Broken glass and foamy liquid spread across the wooden planks. J.B. was at her side almost immediately. He helped her to her feet and then turned to the man who had been harassing her. He grabbed him by the collar of his jacket and pulled him toward the door. Two of the other waitresses began cleaning up the pieces of glass. "You better go take care of your hand. You're bleeding," one of the girls said to her.

In the bathroom, Carly washed her hand and put a paper towel on the cut. She rubbed her arm where the man had grabbed her. It was an all too familiar feeling. The door opened and Lee came in. "Are you okay? I heard you got cut."

"I'm all right, but my clothes are soaked. I need to go back to the motel and change."

"Don't worry about it," Lee said. "Just call it a night."

Carly tried to hold back the tears, but they were now streaming down her face. "I guess I owe you a bunch for that mess," she whimpered.

"Naw, that wasn't your fault. Look, Carly, this kind of work ain't for sissies. You got to get tough if you want to work here."

Carly wiped her eyes. "I guess I'm not as tough as I thought I was."

Lee grinned. "The money is good, but none of the people I hire last very long. You look like a survivor. Just hang in here for a while. Maybe something will come along and change things for you."

Carly wondered what that could possibly be.

CHAPTER FIVE

The motel was not an easy place to live, but with no car, Carly had very few options. It was dirty and noisy with slamming doors and loud music. In the early morning hours when Carly tried to sleep, she would cover her head with a pillow to drown out the voices coming from the adjacent rooms in the motel.

On a steamy Texas night, a couple checked into the next room and argued until daylight. As each hour passed, their voices became louder. It was the unsettling sound of someone being thrown against the wall that made her sit straight up in bed. She ran to the bathroom and turned on the water in the tub to keep from hearing anything else. She had thought about calling the motel office or at least banging on the wall to let them know she could hear them, but she didn't want to start any trouble. Carly heard one last string of profanity and then a door slamming. She peeked out of the curtain and saw a tall man getting into his car. Finally there was silence in the room. Carly swore that by the end of the month she would find a new place to live.

Later that evening at the Double L, Carly pulled her hair up into a ponytail and put on fresh lipstick. Staring into the cracked mirror of the ladies room, she could see the black

The Chester County Boys

circles under her eyes. She felt as if she hadn't even been to bed and Saturday was the busiest night of the week.

"Hey, what's wrong with you, you look pretty rough?" Carly turned to see Nadine Cavinet standing behind her. Carly kept to herself most of the time when she was at work, but Nadine was always friendly and wanted to talk. Nadine twirled her hair with one hand while she chewed a large wad of gum. Her flaming red hair piled atop her head and her large breasts made her look much older than her twenty-one years.

"I'm having a hell of a time sleeping in that motel. I should have enough money by the end of the month to buy a used car and rent an apartment," Carly said.

"You know, Carly, I'm living in a trailer not too far from here. It's not real big, but there are two bedrooms and it would be pretty cheap to live there if you want to move in with me for a while. We could ride together to work. I get real scared leaving here at night all alone. And since Joel left, I'm having a hard time making ends meet. It would really help me out to have someone share the expenses," Nadine said.

"Who is Joel?" Carly asked.

"He and I were engaged, but he got into some trouble with the law and had to leave real quickly," Nadine replied, as she unwrapped another piece of gum.

"What kind of trouble? Is he coming back anytime soon?" Carly asked.

Nadine shook her head. "I haven't heard from him in over a month. It was just some stuff about a car, nothing really big."

"I know I should think about it for a while, but anything would be better than living in the motel. I guess I could give it a try."

After work Nadine drove Carly to the motel to get her things. Carly was anxious. Probably waiting until the end of the month and at least looking at Nadine's place before she said okay would have been a good idea. She should really find out more about this Joel character, but she really wanted out of the motel. Besides it was only temporary. Everything in Carly's life seemed temporary.

Carly stared out of the car window as Nadine maneuvered her car down the dark, gravel road. The trailer park sat in a dusty field four miles out of town. It was a jumbled mass of corrugated steel and rusted metal thrown together as if a Texas twister had dropped it there. Broken toys and bicycles filled the small dirt yards, and loud music filtered from an open door just a few feet away from Nadine's trailer. Once inside, Carly could smell the mustiness of the old wooden paneling and the leaking pipes. A stack of crusty dishes sat in the sink and clothes littered the floor. It was worse than she expected. Nadine gave a nervous laugh as she scooped a pair of jeans off the floor. "I'm not a very good housekeeper."

Carly peered into the spare room. "Damn, I'm not sleeping in here until I clean it up. I'll sleep on the couch tonight." Nadine handed her a scratchy blanket and threw a sheet over the cracked, vinyl couch. "I hope you sleep tonight, Carly."

On Sunday morning, as Carly washed the bedding and cleaned the spare room, Nadine talked incessantly and asked Carly a lot of questions. Carly tried to avoid most of them by changing the subject, but Nadine kept coming back to the same thing. She kept asking Carly personal questions about her life. When Carly didn't answer her, Nadine finally gave up and started talking about work. Nadine said she was afraid of Lee

The Chester County Boys

and she disliked Cletus. He had yelled at her several times because she was always dropping something while the band was playing. He called her stupid and told her if she didn't shape up he was going to have her fired.

"What about Quaid?" Carly asked. "I see him sometimes just sitting on the stage all alone staring into space."

"Quaid is retarded, but don't ever say that in front of Merle. Merle says he's just slow. Quaid loves his music, but Cletus takes advantage of him and teases him a lot. He borrows money from him and then tells Quaid that he paid him back. Quaid never remembers if they did or not. Merle takes care of Quaid and drives him back and forth to work. If it wasn't for Merle I guess Quaid would be in a funny farm someplace. Cletus is a real ass. He drinks all the time, but he still thinks someday he is going to make it big in the music business and play on stage in Nashville. I caught him practicing Elvis moves in front of the mirror in the back and he got real mad. If you ask me, they are all a strange bunch."

"What about you, Nadine? Are you from Lubbock?" Nadine shook her head. "No. I'm, originally from Arkansas, but I haven't been there in years. My dad was a minister and I wasn't allowed to do anything but go to school and church. When my boobs started getting big and the boys started coming around, my dad got real upset and sent me to live with an aunt in Illinois, but that didn't work out either. I'm just like you, Carly. I've had my share of hard knocks in my life. I've lived with four different guys since I left Arkansas and then I met Joel when I was working at the Double L." Nadine stopped for a moment and waited for Carly to shake out the rugs before she began talking again. "When I first met him, I didn't know Joel made his living by stealing. He was really good at it. At first it made me real nervous. I had never stolen anything in my life. He taught me how to shoplift food and clothing, and at night he would hot wire cars and sell them at an underground auction. Somehow he convinced me that we were only taking from people who had too much already and it wouldn't hurt them at all. It was kind of fun. If we needed something, we just went and took it."

Carly sat down on the unmade bed. She couldn't believe what Nadine was telling her.

Nadine continued with her story. "We had a lot of money for a while and then Joel got caught and was sent to prison. Then him and another guy walked away from a work detail. He hid out for about a month and then he came back to see me. The law tracked him right back to the trailer and the sheriff came knocking on my door. Joel jumped out the back window and took off running. I guess he is never coming back. I sure do miss him. Joel was really good in bed and he was a real good cook."

"Hold on just a minute, Nadine. You told me Joel was just in a little trouble. That sounds like pretty big stuff to me. Maybe I shouldn't stay here."

"Oh, no, Carly. Joel is really a good guy. He never killed anybody or even beat anyone up. He wouldn't hurt a flea. Anyway, he would be stupid to come back here, with the sheriff looking for him."

Carly picked up the broom and began to sweep the kitchen floor, again. Nadine jumped up and sat on the counter and started filing her nails.

"What makes you think I have had a lot of hard knocks?" Carly asked.

"I guess I just figured that anyone working at the Double L and living in a motel can't be having a real good string of luck." Carly never answered her. She was hoping that Nadine was right and Joel would stay away from Lubbock. All Carly needed was a little more time and a lot more money and she would be on her way.

CHAPTER SIX

Cletus threw the newspaper down on the bar in front of Lee, tapping his finger on a large ad in the entertainment section. "What's this all about? You never told us anything about an open-mike night. You know how I hate that damn stuff. We tried it once before and it didn't work. I don't want a bunch of drunks spitting in my microphone."

Lee walked over and stood inches from Cletus. "Well, look whose calling the customers drunks. I guess you should know all about that subject. And furthermore, it doesn't matter to me one way or another whether you like the idea or not. I've been putting up with drunks and your ugly face for a long time now. I wanted to go five more, but hey, I can close this joint down right now if business doesn't get better."

Lee had a way of intimidating even the biggest man. She would look them straight in the eye and stare at them, never backing down. With Cletus it was easy. He always caved first. He sat back down on the barstool. "And since when do I need your consent to do anything in my bar? It's just like it says in the ad. Starting Friday night we're going have an open-mike night once a week. I need something to bring more customers into this joint. The competition on this road is getting stiff. Another place just opened up not a mile from here. They got Karaoke."

The Chester County Boys

Lee pushed the paper back toward Cletus. "Here, go show this to Merle." She slid off her stool and started toward her office with a smile on her face. She loved to get the best of Cletus.

Cletus cursed under his breath and grabbed the newspaper off the bar. He hated it when Lee talked to him like he was just another one of her employees. He was a musician and he didn't need her telling him what to do.

After all, the Chester County Boys had been playing at the Double L and bringing in customers for over fifteen years. They deserved some respect. It was Lee who was always changing the rules and he was tired of it. When they first started playing at the Double L it was just him, Merle, and Quaid. Lee got the brilliant idea that they needed a keyboard player. That's when Jack joined them and Randy came a few years later. Just who did she think she was?

The rest of the band grumbled about Lee's decision, but they knew her word was final. They had tried open-mike before and it never worked. People got booed off the stage and an occasional beer bottle landed at their feet. They would just have to wait it out again. A couple of nights and it should be gone. No one was brave enough to face the Double L crowd.

Lee's advertisement in the paper drew a crowd on Friday night. It seemed like everyone was waiting to see who was gullible enough to get up and sing. They were ready to hoot and holler at anyone who tried to take the stage. Carly heard Merle announce several times that anyone was welcome to start off the evening, but no one took the bait. Merle finally said it was time for the band to take a break.

Randy ambled over to the bar and ordered a shot of bourbon. He sat down next to a blonde headed girl who giggled when he smiled at her. She crossed her legs, revealing the top of her thigh beneath her short skirt. He lit a cigarette and winked at her. A tall man edged his way between Randy and the woman. Randy turned around and looked down into his drink. He wasn't in the mood to get into a fight with some bimbo's husband. He yawned. He was tired of playing the drums in this crummy joint every night. Except for getting lucky with the women, there was nothing he liked about it. He glanced over at the bandstand.

Look at them, he thought to himself. Four old men hunkered over their instruments. He sure didn't belong here. When he joined the band he thought he would only be here six months at the most. It was now going on three years.

A couple of the bands he auditioned for before he joined the Chester County Boys told him he wasn't good enough. Maybe they were right. But this job was the pits. It sure wasn't a challenge since they played the same stupid songs and listened to the same corny jokes that Cletus thought were so funny. He was Randy, the high school football star and prom king. He had it all in his hands, until he flunked out of college. Now, he worked days in the automobile factory and nights at the Double L just to pay his rent and keep himself in marijuana.

The man standing next to him left and Randy smiled at the girl again. She giggled and handed him a piece of paper. Randy took it and put it in his pocket. At least he wouldn't be alone tonight.

The band struck a cord and Randy slowly walked across the dance floor and hopped up on the stage; Randy picked up his drumsticks and tapped out a rhythm on the rim of the drum. Jack turned around and gave him a dirty look. It was common knowledge between the employees at the Double L that there was definitely no love lost between Jack and Randy.

The Chester County Boys

Jack constantly referred to Randy as a pothead, or sometimes even worse names. He cursed at Randy for always having to be summoned to the stage when it was time for each set. Randy could usually shrug it off, but there were times when he wanted to just punch Jack in the nose. He believed that Jack was jealous of all the attention he got from the women in the bar.

Randy was right. Jack was very jealous.

Carly went back to the bar for another tray of beer. Lee was standing at the service door drumming her fingers on the shellacked wood. "Damn, this isn't going too good. We got to get someone up there to start this off. The crowd is getting restless. I think a lot of them have left already. How about you, Carly? Can you carry a tune? You go on up there and start things off."

Carly shook her head. "No, thanks, I've got too many customers to take care of. My station is really busy tonight and I can't sing." Lee grabbed her arm. "Listen, I'm not kidding. I'll watch your station, you go sing! Hum if you have too, but do something."

Carly knew this was not a request, but an order. "Please, Lee, don't make me do this."

Lee pointed toward the stage. Carly slowly took off her apron, pushed her hair back from her face and zigzagged her way across the floor to the stage. Her legs were shaking. She really didn't want to do this. She wanted to bolt for the door, but if ten minutes on that stage would allow her to keep her job, she had to do it.

Cletus looked up as she walked toward him. He covered the mike with his hand. "What's going on?"

"I'm going to sing. Lee said I have to get things started. Just play something Patsy Cline."

Cletus nodded. "What's you're last name, Carly?"

"It's Boone, Carly Boone." She could feel the perspiration beginning to trickle down her side. Her mouth grew drier by the second.

Cletus stepped up to the microphone. "Well, folks, looks like we have our first singer of the night. Let's give a warm welcome to our own little waitress, Carly Toone."

"It's Boone," Carly said as she rubbed her sweating palms down the side of her jeans.

The audience began to hoot and whistle as the single spotlight bathed in circles of smoke shone in her eyes. She squinted and adjusted the mike. She waited as Merle fumbled through his list of songs. As the band broke into the introduction to the song, 'Crazy,' she couldn't remember the words.

Her hands clenched the mic, and she prayed she wouldn't pass out. The band struck the first chord over again. Merle leaned in close to her and mouthed the opening lyrics to the song. She stammered for a moment, her voice coming out in a whisper. Someone in the crowd, yelled, "We can't hear you," and there was laughter.

Merle stepped forward. "Come on, Carly, you can do it. Don't let these guys give you a hard time." Carly closed her eyes and began to sing. The words she had learned so long ago came back to her.

Lee watched from behind the bar, as the crowd slowly grew quiet and turned their attention toward the stage. When the song ended, Carly backed away from the mike and the crowd applauded and whistled. She stepped forward and said thank you in a shaky voice. This time they applauded even louder.

"Okay, now it's time for someone else to come up here and sing," Carly said, as she handed the microphone back to Cletus.

Someone in the back of the room stood up and yelled. "I'll be next if you sing one more song." Carly shook her head and hurriedly left the stage.

"That was real good, Carly. You got a nice voice," Lee said. "Starting next Friday you can sing a set with the boys and I'll make up the difference in your tips."

"Thanks, but I would rather just wait on tables. Anyway, the band didn't seem too excited to have me on their stage and, really, I don't want to sing."

"Don't worry about them. I pay for their time, so they don't have anything to say about it. Besides it's better for you to be singing then having to dodge half the men in this bar. You'll make more money, too."

Once again it was happening. Someone was telling her what to do. She could walk away right now, but it would always be the same for her. If she could just stick it out long enough to save a little more money, it would be over soon. But how could she make it through every Friday singing? It would be her worst nightmare.

A few weeks later, on another Friday night after the Double L closed and everyone left, Carly sat at the bar drinking a soda. J.B. had booted the last of the drunks out of the front door and turned off the lights. Carly had never gotten used to the odor of the beer and cigarettes that soaked into her clothes and settled into her hair and tonight the smell was almost making her sick. She wished that Nadine would hurry and clean up her station so that they could leave. She was drained and she needed a shower.

J.B. finished putting the last of the glasses on the shelf. "You got a real good voice, Carly. What are you doing working in this joint? You could be singing in a classier place," he said as he wiped off the bar. "When did you start singing?"

"It's a long story. All I can say is every time I open my mouth to sing, my mother's words echo in my ears. She told me never to sing. To keep my mouth shut and I would be better off."

"Why would she tell you that?" J.B. asked.

Carly shrugged. "That, my friend, is an even longer story."

J.B. leaned on the bar. "I guess you know bartenders are good listeners."

Carly pushed her empty glass toward J.B. and he refilled it with soda. "My mom was a singer. She ended up dead in an alley when I was seven from too many men, too much alcohol and drugs. She said she should have gone to school instead of singing in bars at fifteen and getting pregnant by a man whose face she wouldn't even recognize. Whenever she caught me singing when I was a kid she would put her hand over my mouth. She said she wanted me to make something of myself. So look at me now, working at the Double L and singing to a bunch of drunks."

J.B. smiled. "I know what you mean. I wanted to be a lawyer. Where are you from, Carly?"

Carly hesitated for a minute. "Nowhere, really. Here comes Nadine. See you later."

"What were you two talking about?" Nadine asked.

The Chester County Boys

Carly was used to Nadine's constant barrage of questions. Usually she would put her off, not really wanting to tell her about her private life, but maybe it was time to let her know a few things and then maybe she would stop prying.

"Look, I've got an idea, Nadine. You keep asking me questions about my life. So, let's stop at the All-Night Mart and get some soda. We'll go home and make some popcorn and I'll tell you everything you want to know."

"That sounds great. We can have a pajama party. I'll paint your nails and give you a pedicure," Nadine said, giggling.

Carly rolled her eyes. She was tired of Nadine's constant questions so she might as well give her some answers once and for all.

Later that night in the trailer, Carly took a shower while Nadine made popcorn and turned on the radio. Nadine danced around the room to an old sixties tune. The idea that Carly was going to confide in her made her happy. She had never had a real girl friend.

Nadine put the popcorn bowl in the middle of the bed and handed Carly a soda. She crossed her legs and put her hands on her knees. "Now, Carly, what am I allowed to ask you?"

"Anything you want. But that doesn't mean I'm going to answer you. I can't understand why you're so interested in me."

"Because, you're my friend and I'm nosey. Where did you grow up, Carly?"

"I was born somewhere in Texas, but I spent most of my life in New York. I have no idea who my father is. My mom died when I was seven and I was put in foster homes. I ran away at fifteen and lived on the streets with a bunch of other kids like myself." Carly took a deep breath. "Okay, is that enough information?"

"Oh, my gosh! Were you a prostitute?" Nadine asked.

Carly shook her head. "No. Some of the girls were, but not me. A lot of the kids were on drugs and then there were some just like me. We were just homeless runaways. We did odd jobs to make money, slept in abandoned buildings and kept a low profile. You would be surprised at the number of kids out there. Anyway, when I was seventeen I almost got put in jail for something I didn't do. If it wouldn't have been for the lawyer named LouJean Bailey, I might have been in big trouble. She kept me out of jail and then took me home with her to a place called Ternberry in Massachusetts. I guess that was the closest thing I ever had to a real home."

Nadine got up and poured her soda down the drain and refilled her glass with wine. "Why did she do that for you?"

"I asked the same question, but it took me a long time to believe the answer. You see, LouJean was like the captain of a lifeboat. She rescued drowning people who had lost their way. By the time she put you back in the water you knew how to swim and she knew you were going in the right direction. But, I didn't stick around long enough to find my way. So, I'm still swimming against the current. LouJean was just a genuinely nice person. I wasn't used to anyone doing something for me and not wanting anything in return." Carly lay down on the bed and looked up at the water stained ceiling. "Yeah, I sure messed up. She wanted me to go back to school and then she was going to send me to college. I was so full of anger I didn't give either of us a chance. She knew it and that's why when I left there she didn't try to stop me. She knew I had to find my own way." Carly refilled her glass.

The Chester County Boys

"Wow, that's real sad, Carly. Have you ever thought about going back to see LouJean?"

"Once in a while I did. After I left Ternberry, I went to New York and tried to find some of my old friends. I couldn't find anyone. I rented a one-room dump and figured I could work and go to night school. I wanted to call LouJean and surprise her when I got my GED, but that never happened. I had to work two jobs just to get by."

"Were you singing then, Carly?" Nadine asked.

"I hadn't even given it a thought. I was waiting tables and cleaning offices until I met this fellow named Hobart. He was just a big old county boy trying to make it in the city. Too bad I couldn't fall in love with him, I know he would have been really good to me."

"Oh, man. I've had those kind of relationships. Real bummers," Nadine groaned.

"It wasn't really awful. We shared a lot of laughs and we got along pretty good. I honestly tried to return his affection, but it just wasn't there. Then he decided he needed to move back to Oklahoma to be near his mother. So I left New York with Hobart and we rode together until we got to Kansas. He told me he was hoping to tell his mother that we were getting married, but since that didn't look like it was going to happen, he really couldn't take me home with him. I was relieved. He gave me four hundred dollars and we parted company." Carly yawned. "I'm beat, Nadine. I need to go to bed."

"Wait! You haven't told me about Danny. Where did you meet him?"

"I met him at the restaurant where I was working in Kansas City. We dated for a couple of months and then he moved into my apartment. He was so sweet at first. He rubbed my aching feet at night and brought me roses. He even kept the place reasonably clean. After a while it all changed. He wouldn't work. He ran through all of my money and we lost the apartment. That's when we moved to Sweetwater and he turned into a real son of a bitch. I hate his guts and on that note, I am going to bed."

As the weeks rolled by, Carly began to realize that as much as she tried not to, she did enjoy singing. The crowd still made her nervous, but once she was on stage for a little while she was fine. She was beginning to like the applause and, best of all, she didn't have to wait tables. But, sometimes the words her mother said to her so long ago seemed to echo in her ears. Lee began to put extra money in her pay envelope each week, and the tin box under her bed was beginning to fill up. In a few more weeks, she should be able to give up singing and leave Lubbock. She was still afraid that Danny was out there somewhere looking for her. He didn't give up easily.

CHAPTER SEVEN

Carly was tired. She hadn't slept well all week and her throat was raspy from the thick cigarette smoke in the Double L. Tonight, Nadine decided to stay home from work, saying that she didn't feel good, either. She let Carly borrow her car to go to work. Carly was now singing three sets on Friday and Saturday.

In between sets, Carly helped the other two waitresses cover Nadine's station. After the bar closed, she stopped at the All-Night Mart on her way home and bought groceries. Nadine never shopped, just like she never cleaned or picked up after herself. Carly had a hard time keeping herself awake as she drove home. She turned on the radio and opened the windows.

After parking next to the trailer, she took the bags out of the car. Carly balanced them on her knee as she tried to open the door to the trailer. She pulled on the handle but the door would not open. Putting the bags down, Carly knocked on the door and stepped back.

Nadine came to the door and opened it just a crack. She pulled her robe closed and put her fingers to her lips. "Sssh, be quiet. Joel is here and he's sleeping."

"What do you mean, Joel is here? You said he wouldn't be coming back here. Besides I thought you were sick," Carly said in an irritated voice. "Open the door so I can come in!"

"Sure you can come in. Just be quiet. I don't want him to wake, and don't give me that look, Carly. He is only going to be here until tomorrow. He just stopped by on his way through town," Nadine whispered.

"Well, I want him out of here by tomorrow and I mean it. I should have known you would pull some crap like this. I have to get some sleep."

Nadine went back into her room. Carly washed her face and hands and got into bed. A few minutes later she got up and pushed a chair under the handle of her door.

This night reminded Carly of the many nights when she was a teenager living in New York. She would lie in her bed in the tiny apartment she shared with some of the other street kids and listen to the grunts and moans coming from the other side of the wall whenever some of the girls needed extra money. Tonight was a repeat of those nights. Carly put her pillow over her head to block out the noises coming from Nadine's room and the sound of the flimsy headboard banging against the wall.

Joel was still sleeping when Carly got up to make coffee. She could hear loud snoring coming from the tiny bedroom. Nadine was lying on the couch, her naked body covered with an orange and gold afghan. "I thought you told me you were over him? It sure didn't sound like it last night," Carly said.

"I am over Joel, but I'm not over sex." Nadine turned over and put the afghan over her head. "I just can't stand his snoring."

The Chester County Boys

Carly pulled the plug out of the empty coffee pot, sending small sparks across the counter. "We're out of coffee. You guys just have all the fun you want but he better be gone by the time I get back. Is it all right if I borrow your car again for a while? I'm going in to town and get myself a decent breakfast for a change."

Nadine waved her hand in the air without turning around. Carly took the keys and left. When she was almost to town she thought about her tin box of money under her bed. Maybe she should go back and bring it with her. But Joel was still asleep. He had no idea she had any money and besides she would be back before he woke up.

It had started to rain by the time Carly reached Libby's Café. She ran across the parking lot and shook the water from her hair as she entered the door. Settling into a booth, she looked over the menu. It was Merle who interrupted her thoughts. His head popped up from the booth in front of her. "I thought that was you, Carly. What the heck are you doing in town so early?"

Before she could answer he started talking again. "I'm glad you're here. I was going to ride out and see you today anyway. Lee told me last night that she wants you to start singing with the band every night instead of waiting tables. I guess you know you are really drawing a crowd." Merle slid into the booth with Carly and laid a piece of paper on the table. "I've been working on this list. I figure if you're going to be singing every night we need some new songs. I got a few written down here, but you can add what you want so I can get the music."

Carly didn't have the heart to tell Merle that she probably wouldn't be around much longer. He seemed animated as he talked about the new music.

"I don't know, Merle. I've been singing with you about two months now and in all that time, you're the only one who talks to me. I know Cletus can't stand the idea of me being on stage and Jack just stares at me with those dark brooding eyes. So maybe it's not such a good idea."

"Listen, don't worry about those guys. They'll get over it. Cletus is just jealous and Jack doesn't have a say when it comes to decisions about the band. Anyway, when he has something to say, he'll say it. He's not one for small talk. Hell, he doesn't even talk to me. Jack keeps to himself."

Carly spent the rest of the morning with Merle. They talked about new material and decided to go to the music store and see what they could find. Later that morning, Carly had her hair trimmed and bought a new outfit. She lost track of time and it was almost noon when she started home.

Carly quietly opened the door to the trailer and went to her room to put her packages away. The place was in a shambles. The dresser drawers were pulled out and clothes were slung on the floor. A sickening feeling came over her when she saw the mattress leaning against the wall. Carly frantically threw back the covers that lay on the ground, but she already knew that her money was long gone. Her eyes traveled around the room. The tin box was thrown in the corner. Carly began to scream.

Nadine was sitting up in bed by the time Carly rounded the corner. "God, Carly, what's wrong? You scared the hell out of me," Nadine said pulling the sheet around her.

"Where's Joel? That son of a bitch stole my money and ransacked my room. Where the hell is he?"

Without answer, Nadine leapt from the bed, the sheet falling away from her naked body as she ran to the kitchen counter and opened her purse. "Oh, no, he took my wallet. He's got all my money and my credit card. How could he do this to me?"

"Oh, feel sorry for yourself. I had over two-thousand dollars saved and now it's all gone. Dammit, this makes me so mad!" Carly screamed pounding her fists on the counter.

Nadine walked slowly back to the bedroom. She began to cry. Carly wasn't done screaming at her, but right now the sight of this naked girl sitting on the bed crying didn't make it easy. "I'm so sorry, Carly. I didn't think he would do this to me again," Nadine said sobbing.

The word *again*, stuck in her mind like a barb. How could she have been so stupid to move in with someone she hardly knew? Why had she trusted Nadine? Was it because it wasn't a man this time that screwed her over that made it any easier? It was even worse.

"You can have my car, Carly. I'll get the title for you. I only owe about ten more payments. I may be a little behind right now, and now it looks like I won't have the money to pay it this month."

"Just forget it," Carly said. "We'll have to think of something else to get us through the month. Is the rent on this dump paid?"

Nadine shook her head. "I was planning on going to the office tomorrow. The money was in my wallet. I'm so sorry Carly. I know you hate me now." Nadine sobbed into her hands.

Carly knelt in front of Nadine and put her hands on her shoulders. "Look, it's over and done with. You messed up, but it was just as much my fault for leaving the money here instead of putting it in the bank. All I know is you and I have to get our act together and quit being doormats."

Nadine threw her arms around Carly. "You are my best friend in the whole world. I promise you, I'll pay you back somehow for the money Joel took. Now what are we going to do?"

Carly told Lee that she and Nadine had to quit working at the Double L because they could not find a place to live within walking distance of the bar. Nadine's car was going to be repossessed and Carly refused to go back to living in the motel. Lee begrudgingly told them they could stay in the two rooms behind the Double L. There was only one bedroom and a small kitchenette. Lee had lived there when she first opened the place. Lee couldn't understand why Carly was taking Nadine under her wing, saying that in her opinion, Nadine was a loser and she could easily replace her.

Carly couldn't quite figure out why she was doing it either, except she felt sorry for Nadine and knew how it felt to be kicked in the teeth more than once. Not too long ago she had been called a loser.

CHAPTER EIGHT

Carly decided if she wanted to make more money she would have to take Lee up on her request to sing a few sets with the band every night. They reached an agreement on her salary. Lee grumbled a bit, but she knew that without Carly, business would be back to the usual few customers that showed up during the week.

With new music and new outfits Carly took to the stage each night and gave the audience what they wanted. She sang requests and talked to the people sitting at the front tables. Business began to pick up at the Double L. Carly would still become extremely nervous before each performance. It wasn't until she was on stage singing that she would calm down.

It was Saturday night at the Double L and Carly was in her room getting ready to go on. She held up the red, satin shirt she had bought that day and wondered if she should wear it. In the bar, a man named Wade Upshaw ordered a beer at the bar and ambled across the dance floor to a table near the front of the bandstand. It was only 8:30, but the room was already filling up. He hoped that was a good sign.

He had been on the road for over three weeks now. He got a call that morning from the home office to swing by Lubbock and check out the girl singer at the Double L. All he needed was one more act to fill his roster and he could go home. Wade hoped this was his lucky night. His boss, Jim Colby, had been on his tail all week, wanting to know if he had found someone. Jim just didn't understand. There were a thousand country bands out there, but only a few really good ones.

Wade took a drink of his beer and let out a loud burp. His stomach was killing him. Between the beer and the fast food, his indigestion was really kicking up. As the band members began to filter onto the stage, Wade let out a groan. These guys were older than his headliners. When the music started, he knew that this was just another wasted night. Wade laid a tip on the table and headed for the men's room.

He didn't see Carly go on stage, but he heard her voice coming over the speaker as he stood in front of the urinal. He hurriedly zipped his pants and went back to his table. He picked up his three dollars and stuffed them into his pocket. He signaled to Nadine to bring him another beer.

Maybe this was his lucky night after all. Wade sat through two more sets before he had a chance to speak to Carly. She seemed to disappear as soon as the band took a break. He followed her as she crossed the crowded floor and went to the bar.

Carly ordered a soda and sat down on one of the high stools. She smiled at the people who said hello to her and shook hands with a couple of men. Wade pushed his way through the crowd and sidled up next to her. "You have a real good voice, little lady. My name is Wade Upshaw. I'm with Stellar Productions. If you have a few minutes I'd like to talk to you about a business deal."

Carly gave that knowing nod to J.B. to let him know to be on his toes. He was always fending off pushy men for Carly.

The Chester County Boys

J.B. came down to the end of the bar and rested his hands on the rail. "What can I get you, fella?" he said to Wade.

Wade knew the routine. He pulled out his business card and driver's license and laid it on the bar. "I'm on the level. You can join us if you like," he said.

J.B. picked up the license and held it up to the light. He nodded to Carly. "He's okay. I'll be watching in case you need me."

"I'll be right back," Carly said. "You find a table for us." She circled the dance floor and went out the side door.

Merle was sitting in a chair leaning against the wall. "Merle, I need you. There is some guy out here from Stellar Productions and he wants to talk to me. Will you come with me?"

Before he could answer, Cletus stuck his head around the corner. "What did you say, Stellar Productions? Hell, let's go." He led the way as Carly and Merle followed him back into the bar.

Cletus extended his hand to Wade. "I'm Cletus Hurley. I hear you're interested in our band?"

Wade seemed a bit surprised. He tried to speak, but Cletus interrupted him again. "Yeah, we got a good thing going here, but mind you, it's only temporary." Cletus leaned back in the chair. "Between you and me, we are way too good to be playing in a place like this. So what do you have in mind?"

"As I was trying to say," Wade said, "I'm a booking agent for Stellar and right now we are in the process of setting up a tour to promote an album of some of the stars from the sixties and seventies. It's a grass roots tour called the Jubilee Tour. We got six of the older stars already signed up. Problem is, none of them want to follow each other on stage, so we are putting filler bands between each act. I need one more band."

Cletus grinned. "Keep on talking. We're listening."

"Okay," Wade said. "Here's the deal. It's a fourteen-week tour to twelve different cities. We will be playing in stadiums, county fairs and theaters; any place we can draw a crowd of preferably older fans who remember these guys and will buy their music. We pay the filler bands six thousand dollars a week. You all do the math and split it how you like. You provide your own transportation and lodgings. If you complete the whole tour you get a ten thousand dollar bonus. Each filler band will play two songs. Now I have to scoot back to Tulsa in the morning, so you got until then to decide. I'll leave a copy of the contract and you all can look it over."

Wade stood up. He reached down and took Carly's hand. "And you, Miss Boone, would make a great addition to our tour. I hope to hear from you in the morning." He avoided looking at Cletus.

As he turned to leave, Cletus yelled after him, "Any chance this tour is going to Nashville?" But Wade just kept on walking. He was trying to figure out how he was going to tell his boss that he had hired a real good singer, but most of the band was older than dirt.

Cletus stood up and did a little dance around the table. He was grinning from ear to ear. "Well, I don't know, but I don't think we can pass this up. I admit the money ain't that much, but it's a great opportunity for the band to get out there where we belong instead of spending the rest of our lives in this dump. We need to talk."

The band gathered at Merle's apartment after the Double L closed. Cletus, of course, was ready to quit the

The Chester County Boys

Double L right away. After some discussion, Jack and Randy agreed they wanted to go on the tour. Quaid, of course, had no idea what was going on.

Merle said he had his doubts about the whole idea. "Now look, I know you are all excited about this offer, but let's be practical. Mr. Upshaw was mainly talking to Carly and she hasn't said a word. Second of all, we would have to pay our own expenses, you know, food, motels and transportation. How is that going to work out? I'm the only one that has a truck that will make it more than a hundred miles from here." He crossed his hands over his chest and shook his head. "This ain't the big time guys. We quit our job here we may not find anything as good when the tour is over. What do you think, Carly?"

Carly had been thinking about Wade's offer ever since he left the bar. If she decided to go, it would mean traveling with the band and she still wasn't sure how they felt about her. She had no idea if she would be able to get up on stage and sing in front of a large crowd. She also was afraid the publicity might draw Danny out of his hole. "I don't know. I mean…I don't want to ruin your chances, but like Merle said, it's a lot to think about."

"Hell, Carly, you can't pass this one up. I just knew someone out there was gonna hear you and make you a star," Cletus said. He was trying very hard to convince her for his own selfish reasons. "And Merle, we can always find work." He was now on his feet, pacing back and forth across the tiny living room. "I'm thinking we get a bus. You know one of them big tour buses. That way we won't have to pay for motels and we can even cook some of our own food. And when we pull into a town, we won't look like a hillbilly funeral procession with our old cars and trucks. I know a guy in Houston who has a couple of them for sale. I bet I could get a good deal. I'll go up there and check it out."

Merle stood up and leaned over the table. "Are you nuts? A bus! Who do you think we are, some big time stars? We come pulling up in some big old bus and we'll get laughed off the tour. And besides where in the hell would we get the money to lease a bus. I bet we don't have five hundred dollars between us."

Quaid, who had been sitting quietly, blurted out, "I got money. I got money and I would like to ride in a bus."

"Well, hot damn, that's great! How much money you got Quaid?" Cletus asked in an in a mocking voice.

"Oh, about this much," Quaid said, putting his hand about six inches off the table. "I don't rightly know how much that is."

"No, crap, you really got money, Quaid?" Cletus asked.

"Yeah, I been saving it for a long time. I'd like to ride a bus."

"Now you know everybody, if we take the money from Quaid it is only a loan," Merle said. He turned to Carly. "Okay, darlin, it's up to you. Go or stay?"

Carly took a deep breath. "Go, I guess, but do we really need a bus?"

Cletus slapped his hand on his knee. "Hot damn! We sure do need a bus, Carly. Let's go get your money, Quaid." Cletus grabbed Quaid by the arm and pulled him off the chair.

Merle was irritated. "Hold on just a damn minute. What do you think about getting a bus, Carly?"

"I don't know. Everything is moving too fast. I'm just not sure about any of this. I hadn't planned on being a singer and I…"

The Chester County Boys

Cletus interrupted her. "What! What the hell do you mean?" He was close to her face. "Look, little girl, this is a chance of a lifetime and if we turn it down now, you can kiss your future goodbye. You gonna renege on us? You just said you would go. Besides, we were the ones who gave you a chance to make it to the big time."

Carly was now irritated. "That's all bullshit and you know it, Cletus. I never asked to sing with your band. It was all Lee's idea. If I had my way, I'd still be waiting tables. And I sure don't feel like I made it big. Because everybody else wants to go, I'll go. But stay out of my face, you hear me?"

Cletus softened his tone. "Hey, I'm sorry, Carly. Don't get mad at me. I'm just excited."

Carly spoke again. "Okay, I'll go and I guess a bus would probably be cheaper than leasing a couple of vans and paying for motel rooms every night. I don't have a problem with it as long as everyone agrees that we sell the bus and Quaid gets all of his money back when the tour is over, even if we have to make up the difference out of our bonus." Everyone was in agreement.

"Randy, you go with Cletus. You make sure he doesn't take any more of Quaid's money than he needs. If he does, punch his lights out," Merle said pointing his finger in Cletus' face.

Quaid began to laugh. "That's right, Randy, you punch his lights out."

Cletus held his hand out, wiggling his fingers. "Give me your truck keys, brother."

Merle hesitated for a minute. "I'm warning you, Cletus, you put one dent in my truck and I'm gonna kick your butt."

Merle turned to Carly. "Are you sure you're okay with this, Carly? If you're not, just say so and we'll forget the whole thing."

Carly shrugged. "It's fine. Right now, one place is as good as another. Maybe I can start saving money again. I wonder where Quaid got his money?"

"I'm not really surprised that he has a stash," Merle said. "Hell, he lives downtown in a run down rooming house across the street from me. He doesn't drive and he eats all his meals in a little greasy spoon by his place or we go out to eat together. Once in a while I take him shopping to get new underwear and Levi's. I imagine he spends most of his days either sleeping or watching television until I pick him up to come to the Double L."

"What are you going to tell Lee, if we leave here?" Carly asked.

"I don't know, but it ain't gonna be a pretty scene," Merle replied. "She gets real cranky when things don't go her way. Be prepared for a real tongue-lashing, Carly."

Later that evening, Carly lay in the double bed next to Nadine, in the tiny room. Sleep was evading her. Her mind was filled with what had happened in the last few hours. She hadn't said anything to Nadine. She knew Nadine would go running to Lee.

The thought of going on the road was frightening to her, but living in the dingy two rooms in the back of the Double L for much longer was even more depressing than she could imagine. She was worse off now than when she first came to Lubbock. It seems like she took two steps forward and then one back.

CHAPTER NINE

The next afternoon, Merle loped across the street and stepped onto the porch of his apartment house. He tapped his wet hat on his hand. The raindrops sizzled on the sidewalk still hot from the one-hundred degree temperature. He had taken Quaid to lunch and tried to explain to him what it would be like if they went on the road. Quaid didn't like change and Merle was afraid going on tour would upset him. He wasn't sure if he got through to him or not. All Quaid talked about was riding on the bus.

Merle looked at his watch. Cletus was late as usual. He sat down on the window ledge to wait for his brother. His eyes moved around the room. Merle didn't think he would ever be moving from this place. He had lived here since he started working at the Double L. His threadbare couch and a brown leather chair with duct tape on the arms had occupied the same space in his living room for over fifteen years. Except for his collection of old records, there was nothing in the whole apartment that he even cared about.

A few minutes later, there was a knock on the door. Merle opened it and let Cletus in. "Okay, what's on your mind? Randy and I are anxious to get going."

"Sit down for a minute, Cletus. I need to talk to you."

Cletus rubbed his forehead. "Now what did I do? You gonna give me another lecture about your truck?"

"No, it's nothing like that. I just needed to tell you something before we start this crazy tour. It's been on my mind for over three months now. Now, for once, I want you to keep quiet and just listen to me." Merle hesitated for a moment before he began to talk. "Do you remember back about twenty-five years ago when you decided to quit the band and go off on your own? You and I got in a big argument about that woman you were with at the time. We were in Austin."

"Sure I remember, but what does that have to do with anything? You knew it wasn't my idea to quit the band. It was that gal I was married to at the time. I think it was Rose, or was it Cindy?"

Merle waved his hand. "It ain't got anything to do with you leaving the band. It has to do with me. About a year after you left, Quaid and me were still playing in the same bar. We were doing all right, no great shakes, but we were making it. One night this little gal comes into the bar. She's got a guitar slung over her shoulder and a small girl by the hand. She comes up to me and asks if she can sing a set or two with us. She says she doesn't have any money and she and her kid are living in her van. She has this can she puts on the bandstand that has "tips" written on it. I guess I felt sorry for her. She was so young. After she takes off her jacket, she wraps it around the child and puts her in the booth next to the bandstand. This little gal had a voice like velvet and the people in the bar loved her. They put money in her bucket and she kept on singing. After the evening was over, I took her and her little girl to the Waffle House and bought them breakfast."

The Chester County Boys

Cletus interrupted. "What in the heck is this all about? I'm having a hard time following you. You got anything here to drink?" He got up and went to the refrigerator. Pulling out a beer, he popped the top and slurped the foam off the can.

"Just shut up and listen, okay?" Merle said. "Well anyway her name was Jackie James. That was the name she was using at the time. She started singing with us every night and pretty soon I put her on our payroll. I didn't like the idea that she was living in her van, so I told her that she and her kid could come stay with me. All I had for her was a pull-out couch, but it was better than a mattress in the back of her van."

Cletus grinned. "Okay, I'm getting the picture now."

"No, it was nothing like that. She was just a kid herself, maybe only nineteen or twenty. Hell, I was old enough to be her father. Jackie had a lot of problems. She drank all the time and was messing with drugs. She liked to stay out late and sleep most of the day. I nursed her through an overdose and once when she got beat up, I paid for the hospital. Jackie dated all kinds of men. Most of them were just thugs or bar people. If they gave her money or booze, that was fine with her. She wasn't a very good mother, but, when it came to singing, she had it all together. She said she wasn't sure who the father of her daughter was. Sometimes I would see her playing with her kid and she seemed like a little girl herself; other times it was all up to me to take care of the child. I made sure she had milk and orange juice to drink and I bought her some clothes to wear. Her and I got real close. Sometimes at night when Jackie was out late, I would sit up with the little girl and sing to her. She was only two years old at the time. I would sing, "You Are My Sunshine" to her. It was her favorite song. She started calling me Shine. Her name was Carly."

Cletus' jaw dropped open and he slapped his knee. "Damn, you're telling me that you're the guy Carly has been looking for. The guy named Shine! You have got to be kidding. So Carly Boone was Jackie's kid. I'll be a son of a gun. So why didn't you tell Carly when she asked you right after she started working at the Double L?"

"At first I was just knocked to my knees when I found out that Carly was Jackie's kid and I didn't see any point in telling her. Anyway, Carly and her mom had stayed with me for over two years. Then Jackie got restless. She wanted more of a relationship then I was willing to give her. She took up with this guy named Arliss. He was a small time drug dealer and he convinced Jackie that he could take care of her. I came home one day from the Laundromat and there was a note on the table. It said three words, "I'm moving on." She took all her stuff, all my money and Carly. I tried to find her, but I knew she had left town. I missed them for a long time, especially Carly. But, then I knew I had to put it all behind me and I thought I had dealt with it. That is until Carly showed up. I knew how disappointed she would be when she found out that I was Shine. I sure didn't fit the picture she carried in her mind all those years. I wasn't the big strong man who was going to fight off the dragons and make everything okay. Besides, I don't know why, but I was scared. So I decided I would wait awhile and let her get to know me and then I would tell her. Then Lee started making her sing on stage and I figured she would move on and do okay for herself. Now, we are going off on some crazy tour together."

Cletus shook his head. "Man, that is some story. So what happened to Carly's mother after she left you? Did you ever find her?" he asked.

The Chester County Boys

"No. I got a call one time that she was in jail and I sent money and bailed her out. That's why when Carly told me that her mother died and she ended up in the Welfare System, I just couldn't bring myself to tell her. I really let her down. I should have looked for her, Cletus."

"That's bull, Merle. How in the hell did you know where they went? Didn't Carly say she ended up in New York? Anyway why are you telling me all this now? Were you in love with Carly's mother?"

"I guess in a way I was, but she was so young and so messed up. But, now I have to tell Carly. I can't go on this tour without getting this off my chest. I don't know how she is going to react. She may not want to be around me anymore. That's why I have to tell her before you go off and buy a bus."

"So what are you going to do, tell Carly that her mother was a drunken slut? That should make her feel real good. You're going to screw up everything for us. Damn, I knew something would go wrong."

"I'm gonna lie, Cletus. I'm gonna lie like I've never lied before. I'm gonna tell her how much her mother loved her and that she died because she trusted someone who only wanted to use her. I just hope she understands. Now you go on down to the Double L and wait for me. After I talk to Carly I'll come down there."

"Dammit, Merle, try to make this right. We got a lot at stake here and now it's gonna get all screwed up." He continued to grumble as he left the apartment.

It was one of the hardest things Merle ever had to do. After Cletus left, Merle called Carly and asked her to come over. She was there an hour later.

With Carly sitting in front of him on the worn couch, he took her hands in his. "Carly, I got something I have to tell you."

She listened quietly, her eyes drifting from side to side. When she finally looked into his face, he could see the tears streaming down her cheeks.

"So, if you want to leave right now and never talk to me again, I will understand," Merle said. "But, I just want to let you know that your momma loved you a lot. She did the best she could. She just got mixed up with the wrong type of people."

Her voice was quiet. "Were you ever going to tell me, Merle?"

"Yeah, Carly, I was, but I remember how your eyes used to light up when you talked about Shine. It was like he was bigger than life and here I was, this broken down old guitar player. I couldn't compete with your image of me. I just didn't know how I could ever make it up to you, but if you give me a chance I would like to try. I can't promise you the moon, but maybe we could be friends."

Carly pulled her hands away and put them in her lap. She was silent. Merle didn't know what to do. He waited a few minutes and then stood up. "I'll call Cletus and tell him to forget about going after a bus."

"No, don't do that. I'm just trying to take this all in. I think maybe it would be good if we get away for a while. I have so many questions to ask you, but right now, I can't think of a one. She did love me, didn't she, Shine?"

"She sure did darlin."

Carly asked Merle a hundred or more questions about her mother and their relationship. She wanted to know about the time they spent together and anything he could remember about

The Chester County Boys

her mother. It was as if she was trying to put together the pieces of those few years to create a past she could live with. Each question was answered with a new lie, but Merle was giving her the life she deserved. Merle tried not to go into too much detail. He was afraid she might catch him in a lie. But each explanation he gave her seemed to satisfy her curiosity and she would move on to a new subject.

Merle told Cletus that he hated lying to Carly, but Cletus assured him it was for her own good. Actually, what he meant was that it was for his own good. With Carly and Merle becoming closer, Cletus knew she would never leave the band behind. He was off to Houston to buy a bus leaving Merle with the task of telling Lee that they were all leaving.

When Merle broke the news to her, she was furious. She told him that she knew Carly wouldn't stick around too long, but she didn't expect the band to leave, too. She said there was no way she could find a replacement band on such short notice. Merle knew no one else would work for Lee for as little money as they had for all those years.

CHAPTER TEN

Cletus chewed on the end of a toothpick and walked around the bus sitting in the middle of an over-grown field. He and Randy had driven all the way to Houston early that morning. Cletus figured that Quaid had more than enough money to buy a fully equipped bus as long as it wasn't too expensive. Cletus decided to spend a little more than he planned on. After all, it was Quaid's money and Quaid was excited about riding in the bus.

"I ain't too thrilled about this bus," Cletus said to the heavy-set man standing next to him. "It looks like a pile of rust and has a lot of dents on it. I want a classy bus."

Bud Harbin smiled, revealing a gold front tooth. "Okay, I got some better ones. Let's go back to town."

The minute Cletus saw the bus on Bud's lot, he knew it was the one he wanted. Bud said it was way out of his budget. They haggled for over two hours before Cletus finally decided to buy it. Bud let out a loud belch and rubbed his rotund stomach. "You're killing me, Cletus. My ulcers are kicking up and I need to get something to eat. I'll tell you what I'll do. We'll split the difference."

Cletus turned to Randy and grinned. "You got a deal."

The Chester County Boys

While Cletus and Randy were in Houston buying a bus, Merle decided to help Quaid get his affairs in order and close up both of their apartments. Everything was moving too fast for Quaid, and Merle wanted to make sure he kept him on an even keel. Quaid didn't take change well and he would become stressed. The stress usually meant he couldn't play his fiddle. He would take to talking to himself and rocking back and forth, just like he did when anybody talked about snakes. The idea of riding on a bus was keeping Quaid in a good mood for now. By the end of the week Merle was getting restless. He wondered what Cletus was doing in Houston.

Carly and Merle sat on the small lean-to porch in front of Merle's apartment building, practicing a few new songs they planned to perform on the tour. Carly had enjoyed her time alone with Merle. The idea of going on tour did not seem as scary to her. She felt safe around him. She knew that he would take care of her. Shine always took care of her.
"What do you suppose those two are up to?" Carly asked. "Hell, who knows. If they're not back by tonight, I guess I'll have to go look for them, he said as he lightly strummed his guitar. "I'd sure like to have my truck back."
A few minutes later their conversation was interrupted by a loud honking noise. Merle put his guitar down and hopped off the porch. "Holy crap! Come here, Carly. You're not going to believe this."
Coming around the corner was a large blue bus with Cletus at the wheel. He honked again and stuck his head out of the window. Merle jumped back as Cletus tried to park the bus with two of the wheels going up on the curb. Written in large gold letters across the side of the bus was "The Chester County

Boys Band," and in much smaller letters, the words, "featuring Carly Toone" written in black.

"What in the hell do you call this? You said you were going to buy a tour bus, not a traveling sideshow. Who put this on here?" Merle said pointing to the lettering.

Cletus smiled and removed his new, white Stetson. "I have connections. Isn't it the cat's meow?"

"It looks more like the cat's ass to me. How you going to get that off the bus when we get back from making a fool of ourselves? And by the way, you spelled Carly's name wrong again."

"Look, don't get all excited. I have a plan. This bus is going to help make us famous while we're on tour," Cletus said waving his hat in the air.

"Hell, we'll be able to sell it for twice as much as we paid for it."

Suddenly the whole idea of the tour was amusing to Carly. There was the big blue bus, Cletus in his oversized hat and the fact that she was even considering going on a trip with these five misfits. Carly smiled.

"Yeah, everybody will know about our bus. Just like the Oscar Meyer Weiner Mobile." Merle said, shaking his head.

"I tell you, Carly, Cletus would stand on one foot and whistle Dixie through his pecker if he thought it would make him famous."

It wasn't until Merle entered the bus for the first time that he really began to get angry. "This looks like a rolling bordello. Who in the hell did it belong to?" The inside panels of the bus were painted in shades of pink and the seats were covered in red velvet. At the back of the bus there were two bunks decorated with fringed curtains hanging in front of them.

The Chester County Boys

Cletus could see the angry look on Merle's face. "Look, don't get all riled," Cletus said. "This bus is in real good shape. It belonged to a lady who used to read fortunes. I got a real good deal. You have no idea how much a regulation tour bus cost. A lot more money than we had."

Merle shook his head. "Damn, if I want to be seen in this thing. I think I'll just follow behind in my truck. By the way, where is my truck?"

"Well, we were a little short. Your truck paid for the lettering and gas home," Cletus said as he began to back away. He could see the fire in Merle's eyes. Cletus took off running across the street with Merle on his tail.

"I tried to talk him out of this thing, Carly," Randy said. "But once Cletus had his mind made up he wouldn't have it any other way."

The night before they were to leave on the tour, Carly packed the rest of her clothes and took them to the bus that was now parked in the motel lot across from the Double L. "We want you to have this bed, Carly," Merle said as he carried in her bags to the rear of the bus and opened an accordian door. "That way you'll have some privacy."

"Thanks, I appreciate that. Let's put the rest of the stuff in the holding compartment and go say goodbye to Lee. I know she is mad, but I still want to thank her for all she did for me. I need to say goodbye to Nadine, too."

As Merle and Carly stepped off the bus Nadine was standing by the door.

"Well, hi, darlin," Merle said. "It was nice of you to come tell us goodbye. What's the matter with you? You look like a stray puppy that's just been left on the side of the road? Have you been crying?"

"Take me with you. Please take me with you. I promise I won't eat much and I'll keep the bus clean and do all the cooking." Nadine was sobbing. Carly put her arm around her shoulder. "I just can't stay here alone. If business gets bad I know Lee will fire me and she'll make me move out of the back room and I'm afraid Joel will come back and get me into trouble," she cried. "Besides, Carly, you're my only friend in the whole world."

Merle sat down on the step of the bus. "Well, honey, I know you're sad to see us go, but we're already on a limited budget and I can't figure we can take on another person."

"Maybe I could give her a share of my money. I feel really bad leaving her here alone. Would that be all right?" Carly asked.

Merle shook his head. "If that's what you want, okay. I guess it might be better to have another woman along, rather than you traveling alone with five men."

Nadine threw her arms around Merle's neck and kissed him on the cheek. "Oh, I love you to death. Let me go pack. It won't take me but a minute."

"Something tells me I'm making a big mistake," Carly said.

When Lee saw Nadine going out the door with her suitcase she followed her out to the bus. Standing in the middle of the aisle with her hands on her hips, she stared at them. "So this is what I get for trying to be a nice person. All of you leave at once. Now, I'm short two waitresses and a band. I hope you fall right on your faces and make big fools of yourselves. You can all go to hell, except for you, Carly. I want to wish you good luck."

Jack stood up, "Look, bitch…"

Lee towered over him. She pushed him into the seat. "You don't call me names, Jack Vance. You are one strange bastard and I'm glad to see your ugly face go. You got about as much talent as a trained monkey. I give you about a week before they give you the boot." She turned and stomped off the bus, talking to herself as she crossed the parking lot. Jack watched her in silence. He was raging inside. No one was going to get away with treating him that way. Lee would be sorry. She had put him down for the last time."

"Okay, I guess we better get our act together and hit the road. I got a few things to do, so let's say we meet back here in an hour," Merle said.

Jack started for the door. "I got something to take care of too."

CHAPTER ELEVEN

Thirty miles out of Lubbock, the bus hit something in the road, which flew up and cracked the windshield. Forty miles later, they had a flat tire. It took over four hours to get it fixed causing them to pull into Stannick after the show had already begun. Wade Upshaw was livid, telling them the next time they were late he was firing them and he would sue them for breach of contract. They tried to explain, but he didn't want to hear about it. He had moved the band to last on the program and by the time they began to play, more than half of the people in the audience had left.

Cletus got on the bus and threw his hat down on the bench. "Well ain't that just what we wanted to hear. We get chewed out on our first night on the road. Did he think we were late on purpose? We have got to get organized," he said, tapping his finger on the table. He turned around, "What's that smell?" Cletus began walking down the aisle, sniffing the air like an old bloodhound. He stopped in front of Quaid, who was slumped down in his seat. "Show me the bottom of your boots, Quaid." Quaid held up both his feet. "Damn, that's what I thought, you stepped in dog crap. I told you to be careful when

The Chester County Boys

we crossed the field. I told you all the people from the trailer court walk their dogs back here," he said, handing Quaid a roll of paper towels. "Go outside and clean off your boots."

Quaid tried to tiptoe down the aisle with not much success. Cletus was behind him wiping up the aisle and cursing.

"Well, maybe if you would pay for a parking spot instead of parking way out here in the weeds, we wouldn't have to run like we're crossing a mine field," Jack mumbled.

It was a few minutes later while they rumbled down the road, that Merle asked where Quaid was. He thought he had been sleeping on one of the bunks, but when he realized he wasn't there he got up and came down the aisle. "Where's Quaid? He ain't on the bus." Merle knew Quaid never left the bus alone. Cletus jumped up, "Gosh damn, I sent him outside to clean his boots and he never came back in. Jesus, turn the bus around, Randy. We got to go back." Once back in the field, Cleuts opened the door to see Quaid standing in the parking lot in his stocking feet with his boots in his hand.

"Damn, Quaid, get on this bus! Get on the bus! I swear if you had half a brain you would be dangerous. Sit down and stay there. Now there is a perfect example of why we are so disorganized. We got to deal with idiots for managers and idiots in the band." He sat down, crossed his arms over his chest and pouted.

The next stop was a small town called Ferris. There was a problem with the electrical system and the screeching of the microphones made it impossible for anyone to hear what was going on. The audience began to boo and throw cans and paper cups on the stage. Wade said it was better if they just stopped playing so he could get the system fixed before the next headline act.

It was while they were in Ferris that Merle got the news from J.B. that the night they left Lubbock the Double L caught on fire. The fire charred the two rooms off the back and damaged the stage area. No one was sure how it started, but the fire department had a suspicion that it was caused by some rags that could have been smoldering in the back room for a couple of hours. Merle felt really bad about Lee's bad luck, but Jack was just sorry that the whole place hadn't burnt down.

Two days later they were in Holton and the show was being held in an outside arena. The rain started just minutes after Carly took the stage. By the end of the first number, the thunder and lightning caused everyone to run for cover. Wet and cold, their feet mired in mud, Carly and the boys headed for the bus.

Randy threw his drumsticks down on the floor and began to curse. "This is all bullshit. One more night like this one and I'm going back to Lubbock. Hell, there are more people in Wal-Mart on Saturday night then in these podunk towns. I thought this was a real tour."

Cletus shook the rain from his hat and began wiping it off with a towel. "You get discouraged too easily. We haven't even been on tour for a week yet. Besides, we're still getting paid."

The refrigerator door slammed and Nadine threw an empty bologna package at Cletus. "Well, somebody better do something soon. We don't have a lick of food in this bus. Let's see if we can find someplace to buy some supplies."

"I ain't pulling this bus out of this spot; it took me fifteen minutes to park this sucker," Cletus said. "If you're

The Chester County Boys

hungry go across the street and get a hamburger. Your legs aren't broken."

Cletus was furious when he found out that Nadine was coming along with them on the tour. It took Merle over an hour to calm him down, telling him that Nadine surely would behave and pull her weight. It hadn't happened yet. Carly made her way to the back of the bus and sat down next to Merle who was strumming on his guitar. "Well, aren't we just a happy bunch," she said.

"Honey, this is mild. Wait till they get real mad at each other and start fist fighting."

"You're kidding me, aren't you, Merle? I wish you would have told me that before we started this dumb fiasco," Carly said.

Merle continued to strum his guitar and hum softly. "Don't worry about it, Carly. I was only kidding. It will all work out."

Quaid was the only one who had no problem with the tour. The idea that he could ride on the bus every day made him happy. Except for the performances, he rarely left the bus. He loved sitting by the window and watching the changing scenery. Somehow it made him feel safe. He was hungry. Randy said he would bring him back something to eat.

Randy left to find an open diner, with Nadine running after him in the pouring rain. Cletus pulled his hat down over his head and fell asleep sitting up next to Quaid. It was finally quiet.

"How did you get started in this business, Merle?" Carly asked.

"Well, let's see. Do you want the long version or the short one?"

"Looks like we have a lot of time on our hands so you might as well start from the beginning," Carly replied.

"Cletus and I were raised on a farm outside of Memphis. We lived way out in the middle of nowhere, with no one to play with but each other. It was pretty boring. No television, no telephone, just an old Philco radio to listen to. We would gather around the radio every Saturday night and listen to the Grand Ole Opry. Cletus would grab the broom, pretending it was a mic and belt out all the songs. Mom and dad would laugh and clap. It was kind of fun."

"Then one day we get off the school bus, and we seen this guitar case come bouncing out of the back of a pickup. I guess I was about nine and Cletus was six. We pulled the case out of the road and opened it. It was the most beautiful thing we ever saw. Here's this guitar just shining up at us. We took it and hid it in the shed behind some old burlap sacks and everyday we'd go out and look at it. We would worry that someone was going to come by our house and ask for it back. My dad found it about a week later and made us take it into town and turn it over to the sheriff. I thought Cletus would never stop crying. The sheriff said if no one claimed it, we would be the first one to get to it.

About six weeks later the sheriff showed up at our house with the guitar in his hand. Man, that day was like Christmas in July for me and Cletus. We would rush home everyday from school to see who would get to it first. My dad got so tired of us fighting over it that he bought us an old beat up guitar from the pawn shop, but we still fought over the good one. Cletus decided he was going to become famous and me, well, I just liked playing the guitar. I really had no other plans than to stay in Waverly and become a farmer like my dad. I just wanted to

The Chester County Boys

play the guitar for fun, but Cletus wouldn't give up. He spent his lunch money on old sheet music. Every time he got some extra money he would buy used forty-five records, mostly Elvis Presley, and then he would listen to them over and over again." Merle got up and shifted positions in the seat.

"We would practice every day out in the shed. Quaid had joined the band by then and we started playing together in every saloon and beer joint from Tennessee to Texas as soon as we were old enough. I remember our first gig. We played for a retirement party at the local Elks club. I was standing up on that little platform. My knees were knocking so loud I thought everyone could hear them. When the announcer asked me what we called ourselves, I just shook my head. So, he just grabbed the mic and said, 'Ladies and gentlemen let me introduce you to the boys from Chester County'. The name just stuck with us from then on. Cletus still believes that one day he'll be in Nashville singing at the Grand Ole Opry. You want a drink? I got a bottle of Jack Daniels in my duffel bag."

Merle got up and pulled his bag out from under the seat. He went to the cabinet and took out three glasses. Pouring a little in each glass, he handed one to Quaid, who was staring out the window at the rain. He returned to his seat and handed one to Carly. "Here you go, little girl," Merle said as he sat back down.

Carly took a sip of the whiskey and made a face. "What's with Quaid? Is he related to you?"

"Naw, but I've been taking care of him since he was a kid. Nobody knows what happened to Quaid's momma, but his dad and him lived down the road from us in a little shack. Quaid's old man was a real mean bastard. He hated the idea that Quaid was slow witted. Quaid's dad made his living hunting rattlesnakes. He'd take the skins and sell them for belts and boots. One time I saw him reach right into the crack of a rock and pull a big old rattler out with his bare hands. Quaid was real scared of his dad, but he was even more afraid of those snakes."

Merle peered down the aisle to see if Quaid had heard him, but he was sleeping with his head resting on the window. "I got to be careful. If Quaid heard me mention the word snake, he would freak out. Anyway, one day him and his dad were coming back from a hunt with a big gunnysack full of snakes. His dad put them in the back of the pickup. He made Quaid sit back there in case the law came by. You see hunting rattlers in Tennessee was only legally done about once every three years. He told Quaid if he gave him the signal, he should throw the bag in the weeds. Quaid crawled to the farthest corner of the truck bed and fell asleep. He didn't see the hole in the burlap bag until it was too late. He woke up with rattlers crawling all over him. One of them snakes crawled out and bit him on the foot. Quaid screamed and screamed, but his dad couldn't hear him. By the time they got home, Quaid was unconscious. When he woke up the next day, the doctor had taken off three of his toes to stop the infection. A few days later Quaid ran off into the woods and wouldn't come out. That is, until I went and got him. He refused to go home, so he just stayed with us ever since. His dad said he was glad to be rid of him."

The door of the bus slammed open. Randy and Nadine got on. Cletus and Nadine started arguing as usual. Randy handed Quaid his food and went to the front of the bus. He took the wheel and pulled the bus onto the highway.

Randy hit a bump in the road and Cletus let out a yell. "Dammit, Quaid, you're spilling your drink all over me," Cletus grumbled as he headed toward the bathroom.

The Chester County Boys

Merle continued with his story. "Quaid followed me everywhere and one day when Cletus and I were playing our guitars, he just reached over and took mine. He started playing a song. He didn't want to give me my guitar. So Cletus and me snuck back into his old man's shack and stole his fiddle and gave it to Quaid. He learned to play it in about a week. He's a good old boy, Carly. He's strong as an ox and just as dumb, but I love him. He doesn't have a mean bone in his body and if he likes you, he's your friend for life. Cletus has always been jealous of Quaid. I guess with me being so tall and Quaid such a big guy, it made Cletus feel even shorter that his five foot two inches," Merle laughed. "When we were kids, Quaid used to pick Cletus up and carry him around. It made Cletus so mad. He would yell and scream. Quaid still does it once in awhile just to piss Cletus off. So that's how the three of us got together. I guess you'd better get some sleep." He patted Carly's hand.

"Tell me something, Merle. What would you be doing if you didn't pick up that guitar out of the road?" Carly asked as she stood up.

"I thought of that a lot. Sometimes I wished I would have left it in the road and let the next truck run over it. I guess I would be soaking my hemorrhoids in a tub of hot water after sitting on a tractor every day."

As each day passed, the constant grumbling and fighting going on between Nadine and the guys became worse. Cletus complained that Nadine was eating all the food and drinking his beer. He said she was lazy and that all she did was lay around all day reading tabloid magazines. Randy told Merle that Quaid needed to take a bath because he stunk and wore the same clothes for days at a time. Carly retreated to her bunk to keep from getting in the middle and, as usual, Jack sat sullenly in the back of the bus, saying nothing. Quaid would sit in the same seat, humming to himself and enjoying the ride.

Carly became accustomed to the crowds and began to relax a little. She enjoyed being on the stage each night and singing, even if it was only one or two songs. Slowly the crowds in each town began to warm to her talent and Wade had moved the band to the third slot on the tour.

A few of the other performers began to talk and joke with her as she waited in the wings to go on stage. Her singing was beginning to give her a comfortable feeling that she hadn't felt in a long time. Many nights after her performance, she would sit in the audience and watch the rest of the show even though she knew almost every word by heart. Anything was better than going back to the bus and listening to all the bickering between the others. Carly wanted to scream at them all and tell them to shut up. She contemplated renting a motel some nights, but she didn't want to cause any more friction then there already was.

There were four more weeks left in the tour. Wade Upshaw told Carly that he had talked to Jim Colby, the owner of Stellar Productions, and told him what a good performer she was. He said that Jim had promised him that he would come and take in one of the shows before the tour ended, but he didn't know exactly when. Wade made Carly promise not to tell the other members of the band, especially Cletus.

While the band was getting dressed for another Saturday night show, Wade Upshaw got the message that one of the headliners was sent to the hospital with chest pains. He stuffed his cell phone into his shirt pocket. Cursing, he walked toward the blue bus. Banging on the door, he yelled, "Is anybody awake in there?"

Cletus opened the door buttoning his shirt. "Keep your pants on, Wade, we still got another hour before we go on."

Wade shook his head. "I've got a no-show headliner and I haven't got time to switch everybody's schedule. The auditorium is packed full. It's a sell-out crowd. You guys are going on in about fifteen minutes. Just follow my cue when you get backstage and we'll just have to see what happens."

Wade turned and left before Cletus could say another word, mumbling to himself that he was too old for this crap. Carly scrambled into her clothes and ran a brush through her hair, while the rest of the band got the equipment together. Running across the parking lot, Cletus jumped in the air, clicking the heels of his red boots together. "Hot damn," he yelled.

As they stood against the wall behind the blue velvet curtain, Wade walked into the middle of the stage. Taking the microphone in his hand, he motioned for the house lights to come up. He cleared his throat. "Hi, folks. Glad you all could make it tonight. There has been a little change in the lineup due to the illness of Lou Galloway." There was a roar from the audience. Wade held up his hands. "Now calm down. I'm going to make you an offer. I've got a band with a little singer that will melt your heart. Hell, she sings better than our no-show headliner," he said, laughing nervously. "If you let her sing and you don't like what you hear, I'll give your money back. Now that's fair, don't you think?" The audience clapped and Wade motioned for Carly and the band. As Wade passed Carly, he whispered, "Nothing like a little pressure."

Carly unbuttoned the top two buttons on her black satin blouse and walked onto the stage to a few whistles and catcalls. "Hi, I'm Carly Toone and these are the Chester County boys." She hadn't realized that she had mispronounced her own name.

After the show, Cletus threw his hat on the couch in the bus and slapped Quaid on the back of his head. "We sure kicked some ass tonight. Damn, did you hear that audience applaud? I knew putting those duets in the act would spruce it up. Man, I can't wait to talk to Wade. I bet he moves us into our own spot in the show."

Jack poured himself a half glass of Jack Daniels and sat down. "So you think your moaning in the mic tonight really helped? You are a real dumb ass, Cletus. You should have just let Carly sing by herself. That's what the crowd wanted to hear and besides, Wade has to make sure the audience gets what they pay for and it sure ain't your skinny little ass. And what is with all those Elvis moves? You look like somebody set your crotch on fire."

The next stop on the tour was another small town. A cold rain was falling when they pulled into the parking lot of the auditorium. Cletus bent his head and looked out of the window. "What the hell is this? It looks like a VFW hall. There ain't enough room in that place for a hundred people."

This time Cletus was right. It was just a small auditorium with a sparse audience that seemed disinterested in anyone but the headliners. Wade put them on first and even though Carly gave it her all, they received a lukewarm response.

They packed up their instruments and ran in the rain to the bus. "So, now what are we gonna do? Just sit here and stare at each other. Well, I'm not gonna stay on this bus all night,"

The Chester County Boys

Cletus said, after about an hour of pacing back and forth. "I'm gonna go find someplace to get a drink and have some fun. Anyone want to join me?" No one answered.

Quaid was in his usual seat next to the window. He was curled up in a ball, with a blanket pulled up over his head. Randy was already asleep. Cletus picked up his hat and left, slamming the door behind him.

A few minutes later he returned. "There ain't a damn thing to do is this town. There's only about four streets and they already have the sidewalks rolled up."

He threw his hat on the couch and rifled through Quaid's canvas bag. Pulling out a half bottle of Jack Daniels, he poured himself a stiff drink.

Merle and Carly were still sitting in the front of the bus talking, while Jack sat at the table playing solitaire. Cletus started pacing back and forth again, sipping on his whiskey.

"Cletus, will you sit down. Every time you pass me, you knock my cards," Jack said in an irritated voice.

"Why do you play that stupid game anyway?" Cletus asked. "That's all you do, is play solitaire. What's the point?"

"Long as I'm looking at the cards I don't have to look at your ugly face, now go sit!" Jack growled.

Cletus flopped down next to Merle. "I'm bored. Man, I hate these long evenings. I don't see why we can't have more spots in the show. We're just as good as them old farts that are supposed to be headliners."

Merle chuckled. "They may be a little over the hill, but they still have star-power and people still love them."

"Now, I ain't saying they don't have a little talent but you take Elvis, for instance. He was a real performer. I remember the first time I saw him on stage. I knew that him and me had something in common. That's why I try to pattern myself after him and when I get to Nashville, they'll remember the name, Cletus Hurley. Yeah, me and old Elvis."

Jack let out a howl. "Oh, please. You don't have as much talent in your whole body as Elvis had in his little toe. Just because you're both from Memphis, don't make you kin to him."

"You wouldn't know talent if it came up and hit you in the face," Cletus growled.

"Well, I sure know a load of bull crap when I step in it," Jack replied.

"I'm telling you again, Jack. I've told you this before. My uncle's second wife was a cousin of Elvis Presley. So that makes us kin, once removed."

"Lord, Cletus, you are dumber than a rock."

"What's with you, Jack? You joined the band, what… six, seven years ago and all you do is gripe. Hell, none of us know anything about you, except you never have anything good to say about anything or anybody. You sit up on that stage with that frown on your face like you hate every minute of it. Why do you do it, Jack? What's in it for you?"

"I'm going to bed," Jack said. He threw the cards down on the table and laid down on the bunk beneath Randy.

"That's what I thought. I knew he wouldn't answer my questions," Cletus said. He slumped down in the seat and pulled his hat over his eyes. He would show them. Just wait and see. He would make it big in Nashville.

CHAPTER TWELVE

Danny Reedy opened the door to his mother's house. Before he could even step into the dining room someone yelled, "Well, it's about time."

Danny rounded the corner to see his father sitting at the head of the table with his arms crossed over his chest. "Your mother wouldn't let us eat till you got here and I'm damn hungry. I ain't too fond of cold food."

"I told you to go ahead and eat and not wait for me. I had to stop four times to put water in the radiator just so that junker I'm driving wouldn't catch on fire." He glared at his brother, Ed.

Shirley and Erlene brought the bowls from the kitchen and sat them on the table. Danny gave his mother a kiss on the cheek and took his seat next to her. "What's wrong with your car, Honey?" she asked as she plopped a mound of cabbage onto his plate.

Danny stuffed a biscuit into his mouth. "Ask Ed about it, Mom. He's the one that sold me that hunk of shit. I think you ought to give me my money back or another car," he said pointing his fork at Ed.

"I ain't giving you nothing. That was a good car when I sold it to Carly. And why should I give you the money when she's the one who paid for it?"

"Well, you give it to me and when I see her, I'll give it to her," Danny suggested.

Erlene finally spoke, "What do you mean when you see her? You leave her alone. She hasn't done anything to you. I'm glad she took off."

Danny mocked her, talking in a high-pitched voice. "Leave her alone. Well, she owes me big time. I got my electric and phone cut off a month after she left, then my landlord locked me out of the apartment cause the rent wasn't paid. He won't give me any of my stuff till I pay the back rent. Who does she think she is, sneaking off in the middle of the night?"

"Whose fault is that?" Erlene said. "If you'd get off your lazy ass and get a job like most people you wouldn't have to depend on women to take care of you. I don't blame Carly one bit for leaving you. Who wants to be with someone who is always telling them what to do or pounding on them?"

"Did you hit that girl, Danny?" Shirley asked.

"Hell no, Mom. I never hit her."

"Danny Reedy, you are a big fat liar. You were always hitting on her," Erlene yelled.

"And you, Erlene, are a big fat ass. So shut your mouth. You don't know what you are talking about," Danny answered angrily.

Ed stood up and threw his napkin on the table. "Hey, you watch it, brother. You don't talk to my wife like that unless you want me to pound on you."

Marvin slammed his hand on the table. "Dammit, can't a man eat his dinner in peace!"

The Chester County Boys

Danny pushed his chair back. "I ain't hungry. You guys eat. I'm gonna go outside and have a smoke."

As he headed toward the front door, Danny spied his mother's purse sitting on the coffee table in the living room. Making sure that no one saw him, he quickly picked it up and went into the bathroom. Rifling through it, he cursed to himself. She had three dollars in her wallet and no checkbook. Danny unzipped the side pocket of the purse and pulled out a gas credit card. He smiled. Putting the card in his pocket he crept back into the living room and put the purse on the table. He slammed the front door as if he was coming in and walked back into the dining room. "How long you gonna be here, Ed?" Danny asked.

"Why, you want me to leave?"

"No, I was just wondering if you had anything on your lot that I could afford." Danny looked at his watch. "It's pretty late. Maybe I can come see you tomorrow. Well, I guess I'll go."

Ed stretched his arms over his head and yawned. "Erlene and I are going home. I'm beat. I'll see you tomorrow."

Danny bent down and kissed his mother on the cheek. "I'll call you, Mom," Danny said. He glared at Erlene and left. As he bounded down the steps, his arm caught the base of one of his mother's gnomes that was sitting on the porch ledge. It teetered for a moment and then fell to the concrete. The head rolled slowly down the walk. The noise brought his mother to the door. "Is that you, Danny?"

Danny stuffed the gnome head into his jacket pocket and ran for his car. He didn't want to have any more conversation with his mother. The engine of his car grinded several times before it finally started. He pumped the gas to keep it running and chugged out of the driveway. His mind wandered as he drove and once he had to swerve to stay in his lane.

Cursing to himself, he banged on the wheel. It's all Carly's fault. When he found the little bitch she would be sorry for leaving him. Who did she think she was? Nobody was going to make a fool out of him. Maybe he'd take her up to a cabin somewhere in the woods so they could be all alone. He had to teach her to mind him.

Once in town, Danny circled around the back of Ed's car lot and parked behind the garage. He casually walked toward the cars on the lot with his hands in his pockets, pretending he was just looking. He gave a low whistle when he spied the powder blue Cadillac parked right on the end.

Even though it was Sunday, he wanted to make sure that none of the mechanics were around. Checking out the garage, he bounced up the steps of the office. Danny heaved his weight against the trailer door and it opened with a bang.

Danny knew that even though there were signs all over that the property was under surveillance and had an alarm system, Ed was too cheap to actually have one installed. He opened Ed's desk and pulled out the petty cash box. Inside was several hundred dollars, which he promptly put in his pocket.

Danny replaced the box and shut the drawer. Looking at the board on the wall, he found the key to the powder blue Cadillac. He twirled it around his finger as he walked outside, closing the door behind him. Danny put the key in the ignition of the car. "Come on, baby, you and I are going to Texas." He settled into the front seat and tried to get comfortable. Reaching into his pocket, he pulled out the gnome head and pitched it into the back of the car.

The Chester County Boys

Danny pulled into an all-night gas station and parked in the last island. He put his mother's gasoline card in the pay-atthe-pump slot and stepped around to the rear of the car. He didn't want the clerk to see him, just in case he wanted to check the card and would realize that he was definitely not Shirley Reedy. He hurriedly took the receipt and left the station.

Danny knew his mother would be livid, but she wouldn't call the police on him. He was just a little nervous about Ed. When Ed found the Thunderbird behind the garage, it wouldn't take him long to figure out that it was Danny who broke into his office and took the car and his money. He might think about reporting the theft, but he knew that Danny was wise to his business. Danny knew all about the cars with low odometer readings and fake registrations. And then there were the hyped-up finance charges that were definitely illegal. He wasn't going to waste his time worrying about his big brother.

Around midnight Danny began to get sleepy. He turned the air-conditioner up full blast and flipped on the radio. Nothing helped him, he was just too tired. He had to stop.

Danny pulled into the parking lot of White Castle and went inside. He ordered six hamburgers, heavy on the onions, and two large fries. He quickly downed a large soda and asked for a refill. Taking his order he slid into a booth and began to devour the hamburgers.

Someone had left the morning paper on the table and he opened it to the comics. Eating the last of the burgers, he turned the page while he finished off the fries. Staring him right in the face on the entertainment page was Carly's picture. Danny sat straight up and folded the page in half. "Well, I'll be damn," he said out loud, drawing attention from the couple at the next table.

The article was an advertisement for the final show of the Jubilee Tour to be performed in Tulsa on Saturday night. Each performer had a small write up and their picture next to it. Danny read the article twice wondering who the Chester County Boys were.

Well, well, Carly Boone. You're gonna have a surprise visitor in the audience this Saturday night. Danny tucked the paper under his arm and left. Tulsa was only a couple hundred miles away. He could take his good old time.

CHAPTER THIRTEEN

Carly had no idea that Jim Colby had been in the audience the night she sang for the no-show headliner. He sat in the back of the auditorium where no one could see him. He couldn't take his eyes off of her. He couldn't put his finger on it, but it was something about the way she delivered a song that made you feel like she was singing only to you. He watched the show and left without introducing himself. Later that week, Jim called Wade Upshaw and told him he wanted him to have a meeting with Carly the following morning at ten.

When Wade told Carly that Jim wanted to see her, Cletus immediately chimed in and wanted all the details. "Now look here, Cletus. All I know is that he wants to see her and just her. He didn't say anything about you coming along."

Cletus started to say something else but Merle interrupted. "I'll drive you into Tulsa and wait in the car for you. Cletus, you are staying here!" he said pointing his finger in Cletus's face, "I mean it. You are staying here!"

Later that evening, after Carly had gone to bed, a soft tapping awakened her. Putting on her robe, she padded across the floor and opened the door just an inch. "Who is it?" she asked.

"It's me, Cletus. I really need to talk to you. It's real important."

Carly opened the door and flicked on the light. "Can't it wait till tomorrow, I'm really tired?"

"Please, it will only take a minute." Before she could answer, Cletus stepped into her room and closed the door. "Listen, Carly, I know I haven't always been the nicest person to you, but you know I like you a lot. I want to ask you a favor, a real big favor. In fact, I'm even gonna beg if I have to. It's about your meeting tomorrow with Jim. I want you to tell him that the band has to be part of any deal you make with him. It's our last shot, Carly. It's either now or never. I want to do it, especially for Merle. He wants this real bad. It would mean a lot to him and of course, to me, too. So like I said, I'm begging. Please."

Carly just stared at him. She had no idea what to say. She stammered. "I think you're lying to me. Merle never mentioned a thing to me about wanting to go on another tour."

"Okay, okay, maybe I exaggerated a little bit. It's important to Jack, and me, too. I'm begging you, Carly." She stared at him. He seemed so pathetic.

"I'll ask, Cletus. That's all I can do, but I can't guarantee anything."

Cletus grinned. He grabbed her hand and pumped it up and down. "Thanks, Carly, thanks a lot."

The next morning Carly arrived right on time at Jim's office. He opened the door for her and gestured toward the leather chair in front of the desk. He glanced at her as he circled the desk. She looked good. She wore black jeans and a pink sweater. Her hair hung loosely around her shoulders.

The Chester County Boys

Jim sat down and tapped the pencil on the desk. "What do you know about Stellar Productions, Carly?"

She shook her head. "Just that you were the people that produced the Jubilee Tour."

"Well, it is not *people*, it's only me. I own this company lock, stock and barrel. I have no partners and no shareholders. It is all mine," he said with conviction. "I do two things. First, I promote tours. These older performers can still put on a good show and for a lot less than some of the newer stars. Yes, the Jubilee Tour has made me a lot of money. The second thing I do is look for new talent. Not just anybody. I have to know right from the start that they are going to make it in this business or I don't even give them a second look."

He leaned forward, looking her straight in the eye, "You, my dear, have that quality. Tell me about yourself, Carly."

Carly stammered. "What do you want to know? You ask the questions and I'll give you the answers."

"I like your style," he said. "What is your musical background? Do you have a manager?"

"No musical background whatsoever and no I don't have a manager," she replied. "I also don't have a husband, no kids or a boyfriend, if that was your next question."

The phone rang and Jim reached over and picked it up. He put his hand over the receiver. "I've been expecting this call. I'll be with you in a minute."

Carly looked around the room. It was dark and cool, decorated in leather and ornate wood. It looked expensive to her. One wall covered in glass held an array of awards and gold records. Carly thought to herself that Jim probably was amazed when she told him she had never heard of his company.

"Sorry about that," Jim said. "It was an important call. Now, where were we? What I propose is a one-year contract. It would probably include one single, one album and a tour. I would be in complete charge of your career during that time. Does that sound fair?"

"I guess, but can I have a few days to think about it?" she asked as she rose from her chair.

Jim stood up. "Sure, get back to me by Friday." He put his hand on her back and escorted her to the door. He watched her as she waited for the elevator. She turned and smiled at him. Yes, he liked her. It was going to be a good relationship.

Carly and Merle poured over the contract lying on the table. She stood up and rubbed her head. "I don't know, Merle. What do you think? Everything is just moving too fast for me. I mean, I'm still excited about this tour and now I have something else to consider. What do you think Merle? Maybe I need an agent or a lawyer before I sign these?"

"Do what you think is best for you, darlin. That's all that matters. This may be your one and only shot at the big time, so if that's what you want, you'd better grab it. These offers don't come along every day, but if you still have some doubts, say no right now and be done with it."

"I can't do it alone. I want you to come with me."

"Well, darlin, I know that is probably not part of the bargain, but I'll do anything you want."

After much deliberation, Carly finally decided to go with Jim Colby if he would include the band in the contract. She knew he wouldn't take Merle by himself, but he might consider the whole band. Jim was shocked at her request. She tried to explain her reasoning to him, but it didn't make much sense. It

The Chester County Boys

was only after several phone calls that Jim agreed. If it were the only way he could get Carly then he would take them too. He would figure out a way to get rid of them soon.

On their first meeting as a group, Jim told Cletus that he should have the bus painted a more demure color. "This is not a carnival act. I don't need my performers riding around in something that looks like it was designed for a bunch of clowns."

Cletus was offended and Jim knew dealing with him was not going to be easy, especially since Cletus felt that he was still the star of the show. No matter how much Jim tried to convince Cletus that he was really showcasing Carly, Cletus just rambled on about costumes and lighting and wanting to know if they were going to play in Nashville.

Cletus wasn't satisfied and said they needed some more of his demands in writing. He wanted a new bus and more money. It was only when Merle realized that Jim was getting irritated that he told Cletus to back off for a while. Cletus begrudgingly did so. Yet days later, Jim presented the band with a written contract that they all eagerly signed. He was glad they did not read the small print, which stated that he could cancel their contract at any time.

CHAPTER FOURTEEN

On the night of their final performance with the Jubilee Tour in Tulsa, a party was planned for all of the performers after the show. Wade had packed his bags and taken them to his car. He went to the bus to make sure everything was okay and to pay Carly and the band. Merle took the check for ten-thousand dollars and shook his hand. "It's been real nice doing business with you, Wade. You're an honest man and we appreciate all you've done for us."

"Well, now that Jim has decided to take over the managing of you guys, I won't be seeing much of you. I'm going to leave now, so I hope your last performance is a good one. If I was twenty years younger, I'd represent you myself, but I don't need any more headaches." Wade wished them well and said he would see them at the party.

Cletus came out of the bathroom dressed in a new white fringed shirt just as Wade was leaving. Rubbing his boots on the back of his pant leg he motioned to Merle. "When can I have my money?"

"You'll get it when I cash the check and we take care of paying Quaid."

"Well, you better wake up Quaid and get him ready," Cletus said.

The Chester County Boys

Cletus had become increasingly annoyed with Quaid. He really wanted to talk to Merle about replacing him. "Let's say we have to do an interview sometime, he'll probably make an ass of himself and embarrass us all," Cletus said, but Merle would not hear of replacing Quaid.

All of the performers were in high gear for the last night of the tour. The audience applauded and yelled and each act made sure they gave at least two encores. Cletus went to the dressing rooms to get himself a drink while they waited to go on. Minutes later he bounded up the steps breathless and grabbed Jack by the arm. "Come here quick, I have to tell you something."

"This better be important," Jack grumbled. "We're due to go on in about five minutes."

"He's here. That guy that Carly ran away from is in the audience. And big mouth Nadine told him everything. She told him all about Carly and about her new contract. We have to do something quick before he gets to Carly."

"How does Nadine know it's him? She never met him before," Jack asked.

"She was standing at the back of the audience like she does every night and he happened to be standing next to her. You know, Nadine, she would flirt with a blind man if she thought they would buy her a drink. Besides, she likes to make people think she is part of the troupe. She struck up a conversation with him and when he started asking lots of questions about Carly, she told him all he wanted to know before he slipped up and told Nadine that he used to date Carly. It didn't take Nadine too much longer to figure out that he was Danny. She got scared and came and told me. If Carly finds out he's here, she'll probably make a run for it and there goes everything."

Even though Carly had asked Nadine not to tell the boys about Danny, she couldn't keep the story to herself. Not only did she tell them, but also added her own embellishments to Carly's story. She said he carried a gun and wasn't afraid to use it.

"Maybe we can just get him aside and talk to him. Tell him to leave Carly alone. You know, kind of scare him a little bit," Cletus said.

Jack thought for a moment before he answered. "Listen, we don't want any trouble but I don't think just talking to him is gonna make him leave. Make sure he stays away from Carly. Just keep an eye on him. If he makes a move toward her, let me know."

Jack found Nadine and pulled her aside. "After we get off stage I want you to keep Merle and Carly busy. If they ask where the rest of us are, just tell them we went back to the bus to smoke a joint and we'll be back to the party later. That's the least you can do."

Within minutes, Jack had devised a plan that would take care of Danny without Carly or Merle knowing anything about it. He gave Cletus some simple instructions.

After their last set, Cletus went out to the parking lot and pulled the car he had borrowed from one of the other band members around to the back door. A few minutes later, Jack and Quaid came out of the stage door with Danny between them, kicking and cursing. Quaid threw him into the back seat and sat on him, while Jack got in the other side.

The Chester County Boys

"You son of a bitch, get off me! What the hell do you guys think you're doing?" Danny screamed, as he wriggled and twisted.

Jack tossed a roll of duck tape across the seat. "Here, help me shut his damn mouth. Tape his hands and feet, too."

"Where was he?" Cletus asked. "Did he talk to Carly?"

"We found him hiding behind the stage," Jack said. "We got to him before anybody saw us. Carly wasn't anywhere around."

Quaid held Danny down, while Jack put duct tape over his mouth and bound his hands behind his back. All the while, Danny struggled and kicked.

Cletus pulled the car out of the parking lot and onto the road. "Now what? Where should we take him to have our little talk?"

Jack leaned forward in the seat. "There's a park up the road about three miles. I saw the sign this morning. Turn left at the next stop sign."

Cletus maneuvered the car along the unfamiliar roads of the park, following the signs leading to the top of a bluff.

Danny's eyes darted from Jack to Quaid. as he struggled to free himself.

"Why are we doing this Cletus?" Quaid asked. "Why we taking this guy for a talk?"

"He's a bad man, Quaid. He wants to hurt Carly. We can't have that, can we? You like Carly, don't you, Quaid?"

Quaid nodded. "I like Carly a lot. She's my friend. He better not hurt her."

"Well, we're gonna make sure of that," Cletus said. He pulled the car into a small parking area and stopped. A single light illuminated the path leading to the small slab of concrete marked 'scenic view.'

Jack got out of the car pulling Danny out behind him. He motioned for Quaid to follow him. "You stay here, Cletus. Keep the motor running and if anyone shows up, flash the lights at us. Danny and I need to have a little chat."

"Why do I have to stay here? You stay. I'll talk to Danny."

"Look, stupid. I said stay here!" Jack growled.

Even though Cletus had never told anyone, he was afraid of Jack. Jack had a way of intimidating him.

Jack and Quaid carried Danny across the grassy area, past the stonewall of the scenic viewing area to the edge of the precipice. "Now this is what we want you to do, Danny, if you know what's good for you. When and if you get back to the auditorium we want you to get in your car and get as far away from Carly as you can and that way nobody gets hurt, especially you. If you think I'm kidding, just try me. Now I'm going to take the tape off of your mouth and you can tell me if you agree with me," Jack said as he ripped the tape from Danny's face.

Danny let out a yell. "Dammit! That hurt. I don't know who you are but when I get myself free from you, I am going to kick your ass and then I'll deal with your buddies. Carly belongs to me and I'm the one who got left behind. Cut this damn tape off my hands right now!"

Jack pushed Danny's face into the ground. "We're going to have to teach you some manners and show you that we mean business."

He pushed Danny's head near the edge of the rock facing. With Danny's head dangling slightly over the edge, Jack told Quaid to grab hold of his legs. A stream of profanity escaped from Danny's mouth as his body writhed back and forth pushing him closer to the rim.

He struggled to free his hands, the tape getting looser. The dew-covered ground beneath him was slippery. Danny's body inched further down the muddy slope as rocks and clumps of dirt began to tumble down the steep embankment.

He was now hanging almost completely over the edge of the cliff with Quaid struggling to hold his legs as his feet dug into the wet grass. Danny let out a scream as his body inched further down.

"Now we can either pull you back or let go. It's your choice. Are you going to leave here tonight?" Jack asked.

"Okay, okay. I'll leave. Pull me back in!" Danny yelled in a frightened voice. His eyes widened. "Pull me in, now!"

Quaid tried to reposition his aching legs, his arms quivering from the weight of Danny's body dangling below him. "I can't hold on any longer. I'm losing my grip, Jack!" Quaid yelled.

Danny's body gyrated in a full turn as he slipped downward. Jack stumbled over uaid's feet trying to get to Danny. Quaid fell backwards into the mud as his hands slipped away from Danny's legs.

"Jesus!" Jack yelled as he dove forward and grabbed the cuffs of Danny's pants with both hands.

Now Danny's body was swinging back and forth, crashing into the rocks on the cliff side. As one of his hands came loose from the tape he clawed at the air. His hand reached up and grabbed Jack's hair. Jack let out a yell as Danny's grasp pulled a tuft of hair from his scalp. Jack let go of Danny's pant leg and grabbed his head with one hand. Jack could see the horrified look on Danny's face as a gurgling noise escaped from his throat. Jack grabbed at the air, but it was too late. He could see on Danny's face as his body slipped into the darkness below. Jack never heard a sound but he knew that Danny must have landed somewhere far below in the canyon.

"Oh, my God, what in the hell did you do, Quaid? Why did you let go of him? Now look what you did!"

"I didn't do anything," Quaid said in a frightened voice. "I didn't do anything. I just did what you told me to do. I couldn't hold him anymore. Maybe you better go down there and see if he is okay."

Jack let out a cynical laugh. "Hell, I'm sure he's just fine. I mean, who wouldn't be after falling about a couple of hundred feet straight down? Come on let's go."

Quaid stood for a moment looking over the bluff. "It was an accident, Jack. We didn't mean to hurt him that bad. If we call Merle we can tell him it was an accident and he was gonna hurt Carly."

"Yeah, sure, dummy. He just happened to fall over the edge of a cliff with duct tape hanging on him. I'm sure they would believe us."

Jack turned and started back toward the car with Quaid slowly following behind him. "Now listen to me, Quaid. You don't say nothing, you hear. Not a word. You let me o the talking."

"Where's Danny? What was all that screaming about?" Cletus asked as Jack opened the car door. "I was afraid somebody was gonna hear you guys. You're getting mud all over the car."

"He got away from us, but I gave him a good scare. I don't think he'll be bothering Carly anymore. Isn't that right, Quaid?" Jack asked, his eyes narrowing as he glared at Quaid.

The Chester County Boys

"Tell Cletus how Danny got away from us and ran into the woods."

"He got away from us." Quaid sat slumped in the seat, with his hands quivering.

"We're going to go back to the party and pretend this never happened. There's no need for Merle and Carly to know about this. Let's just keep our mouths shut. Okay?" Jack said, poking at Quaid.

"Hey, I couldn't agree with you more. Whew, that was a close one. I'm glad that bastard took off. Now let's go party," Cletus said.

The owner of the motel where Danny was staying waited four days before he called a friend of his. He said that he had been stiffed for rent on the room, but the guy left his car. Two days later a tow truck arrived. The driver handed the motel owner an envelope filled with cash and drove away.

Just like most of the cars on Ed Reedy's used-car lot, the powder-blue Cadillac got a new red paint job and new registration.

Later that week, Cletus took part of his money from the tour and bought a red Cadillac. It was in perfect condition. Not a dent on it and very low mileage. No one had noticed that there was a gnome head wedged under the front seat.

CHAPTER FIFTEEN

Jim Colby slammed his hand down on the table, causing Carly to jump and step back from the microphone.

"How many times are we going to have to go over this same damn song before you get it right?" Jim yelled in an irritated voice. "What key are you playing in, Cletus? And Quaid, I don't even think you're on the same page. I didn't bring you all here to make an ass out of me. Now get your act together and learn the damn music. I'll be back later," he said as he strode across the room.

Cletus put his guitar in its case and snapped it shut. "That's gonna do me in for today. I'm going to get a drink." He hurried after Jim, calling to him as he turned the corner.

"Jim, wait up. I wanted to talk to you a minute. I was just thinking, since you're letting Carly make a single before we start the tour, why not let us boys cut one of our own? You know, kind of showcase our talent."

Jim wiped his brow. "Cletus the only talent you and the boys have right now is taking up space. Go back and practice some more."

A lot had happened since they had arrived in Tulsa two weeks prior. Jim decided that in order to save money it would be best if he could find some place where they all could stay together. He rented a spacious house for them on the outskirts of town. Carly was thrilled to sleep in a real bed, in a room of her own. He set up a rehearsal studio on the first floor, renting sound and recording equipment. He was fastidious in everything he did. He kept a record of all of their expenses and told Carly that he expected to be repaid when they started making money. Jim also told Carly that he did not intend to pay for Nadine's expenses since she was not a member of the group.

The relationship between Nadine and Carly had slowly begun to deteriorate. Carly caught Nadine in several lies and also was missing some of her clothing. When she asked Nadine if she had taken them, Nadine said no and that she was hurt that Carly would even think she would do such a thing. Several days later, Carly found some of her things hidden in the hall closet of the bus.

Nadine was lazy. She slept, ate and read magazines most of the time. Whenever anyone asked her to do something for them, she would whine and say she didn't feel good. Nadine was forever borrowing money from Carly for cigarettes and food. She was on a constant manhunt, telling Carly about all the men who were lusting after her.

Carly wanted to tell Nadine things were just not working out anymore and it would be best if she went back to Texas, but Carly hadn't found the courage to do it. Nadine was always telling Carly what a good friend she was and how happy she was to be with her. Carly's problem was solved on the day they moved into the house.

Cletus and Nadine got into a heated argument when Nadine insisted on having her own bedroom, leaving only four for the men to share. None of the men wanted to share a room. Standing only inches away from each other, Cletus yelled and cursed telling Nadine that she was nothing but a lazy cow and she was always trying to cause trouble between him and the other members of the band. He told her that she had a big mouth and no class and he wanted her out of his sight. When Nadine turned to the other members of the band for support, none was given. It seemed that everyone felt the same way.

Nadine stormed out of the house and didn't return until the next morning. She told Carly that she had found a job in a restaurant in Tulsa and just needed some money to rent an apartment. Nadine cried, saying she couldn't stand being treated so badly by Jack and Cletus. Carly gave her five hundred dollars and breathed a sigh of relief.

That evening after Nadine left, Carly sat up in bed and listened to the sound of a train whistle coming from somewhere off in the distance. Even with all that was going on in her life she still felt alone. It was the same feeling she had many times in her young life when her mother would leave her with some friend or neighbor that Carly hardly knew.

After she ran away from her foster home, there were times in New York when she slept in boxcars. When the weather turned frigid, she would seek out the group of kids living in one of the abandoned warehouses. Carly would curl up next to some strangers just to keep warm.

Sometimes she would think she might be better off back in one of the foster homes. Then she would remember how scared she was that maybe her foster father or brother would open the door and come into her room in the middle of the night. Just remembering that feeling made her nauseous. She told herself over and over that she would make it one way or another. She never knew it would be singing that would change her life forever.

She sat on the edge of bed, the song she had been rehearsing earlier in the day running through her mind. She

The Chester County Boys

wondered if Jim was mad at her too. He hadn't said anything to her, but he sure was upset. Putting on her robe and slippers she quietly walked down the hallway to the kitchen. A stream of light shone from under the swinging door.

Slowly pushing open the door, Carly peeked in. Merle sat at the table eating a sandwich. He looked up as she entered. "Hi, what are you doing up? Are you hungry? There's a lot of good food in the refrigerator."

"Not really. I just couldn't sleep. How come you're up, Merle?"

"Well, darlin, to tell you the truth I've been sitting here thinking about Quaid. He is acting real strange. Or should I say, stranger than usual. He keeps asking me about Hell. He said there were probably snakes in Hell and he just couldn't go there. He walks the floor at night and several times I heard him talking to himself in the bathroom." Merle took a bite of his sandwich and shook his head. "He can't even keep his mind on his music. I just don't know what to do. It just ain't like him. I think the change has really upset him. I just might have to send him home to Lubbock."

Carly poured herself a glass of milk and sat down at the table. "Are you sure it's just the change? He seemed okay on the last tour. Maybe he doesn't like living in this house since it has that big field out back. He asked me the other day if I thought there were any snakes out there and I told him no."

"That's a thought, but I keep feeling like it's bigger than that. Quaid hasn't brought up anything about snakes in years. I can't understand why it would bother him all of a sudden. I got to find out what's going on before he really goes off the deep end."

Carly looked into Merle's eyes and she could tell he was really worried. She liked him a lot. There were times when she felt so very close to him. Maybe it was because they were both loners.

Merle wasn't the only one concerned about Quaid. Jack was too. Quaid had come to Jack several times saying he wanted to tell Merle about what happened on the bluff. Jack tried to convince Quaid to keep his mouth shut. He said that if he told, Merle would be really mad and not like him anymore, but Quaid insisted that Merle was his best friend and he could fix what had happened.

In desperation, Jack said that if anyone knew about what happened Quaid would probably go to hell and have to spend the rest of eternity surrounded by rattlesnakes. Just the thought of the snakes made Quaid swear he would never say a word to Merle about Danny's death.

Jack decided it was time to put a little more pressure on Quaid. He would have to handle this one on his own. Jack disliked being involved with Cletus. He hated the little twerp. He knew that eventually he would have to take care of him, but right now, Quaid was the one causing the trouble.

Jack always kept to himself. His past was nobody's business. It was his secret to keep forever. Jack had kept himself out of trouble for the last seven years and now it was happening all over again. The best thing to do was probably pack up his things and leave, but he wanted to be with the band when they finally hit the big time. They were too close to give it up now. He never let on, but he wanted it more than the others could imagine. Jack cared nothing at all about being famous; he wanted the money from the residuals so he could start a new life somewhere else. Then he would get even with all those people who had treated him badly.

The Chester County Boys

❧ ❧ ❧ ❧

JJack Vance was not his real name. He was born Robert Bedermann in Newark, New Jersey to a domineering mother and a spineless father. He was the funny looking Jewish boy who wore a beanie to school and was teased by his classmates. Even in high school, things were not much better. With his face covered with acne and his Yarmulke on his head he was constantly the butt of everyone's jokes. He didn't get along with the other students or the faculty. After being made fun of by a teacher in front of the class, he flew into a fit of rage and pushed the teacher into the blackboard. She should never have gotten in his face. He was always being accused of something he didn't do. The school board wanted to put him in a special class for kids with disciplinary problems but he refused and quit school at sixteen.

The army wasn't the answer either. Robert Bedermann was given a dishonorable discharge because he couldn't follow the rules. Again it wasn't his fault. The rules were stupid and the non-coms were idiots. He was glad they let him out after only six months.

After the army, he had a series of jobs: night watchman, furniture delivery man, landscaper, and on and on. His employers just didn't appreciate him. So what if he got a little pissed off now and then. Was that any reason to fire him? One in particular got in his face and he had no choice but to punch him.

It was after he served three months in jail for assault and battery that he decided it was time to get out of New Jersey. He moved to Las Vegas and found a job in a casino running a roulette table. Everything was going good for a couple of months and then it happened. No one is supposed to touch the wheel but the operator. Why did the man keep sticking his hand out and rubbing the wheel for good luck? The man was told to stop but he wouldn't. He really didn't mean to hit the guy that hard and how was he supposed to know the s.o.b. had a heart condition. It was a short trial. He was sentenced to serve seven to twelve years in prison for manslaughter.

He probably would have gotten out in five, but every fight with another inmate added six months to his sentence. It was those fights and his violent temper that kept him from being pushed up against the cold tiles of a bathroom stall by someone twice his size. Nine years and thirty-one days after he first entered prison, Robert Bedermann escaped, leaving a guard dying on the concrete floor of the gym. Two days later Robert Bedermann ceased to exist. He was now Jack Vance from Houston, Texas; no one would ever call him Robert Bedermann again. He had learned four things in prison: how to forge documents, how to play the keyboard, not to trust anyone and to keep his mouth shut. He planned on using all of those things to start a new life.

His new identity cost him the five-thousand dollars he had extorted from other prisoners. He now had an untraceable past, with a new social security number and birth certificate. Three months later, he had a new trimmed down nose and thirty pounds less on his body.

Jack moved to Texas to start fresh. He joined the Chester County Boys in Lubbock and rented a small apartment. It wasn't much of a life, but for the first time, nobody was pushing him around or getting in his face.

The Chester County Boys

His new demeanor kept everyone at arm's length. Jack knew that he made people uncomfortable when he stared at them with his cold eyes, and he liked that feeling. The idea that people were actually afraid of him gave him a level of control that he reveled in. He hated country music. He hated the twangy songs about men who lost their dogs, their wives and their trucks but it was a good cover. No one would ever expect Robert Bedermann to be playing in a country band. Carly was his only ticket to the top, and he would make sure that Quaid or anyone else who got in his way paid dearly. Killing Danny, had been an accident. But it was an accident no one would ever pin on him.

❦ ❦ ❦ ❦

The next morning, Merle heard Quaid screaming again. Merle ran out of the bathroom with shaving cream on his face and into Quaid's room. Quaid was standing on the bed shaking, his back against the wall.

"What's going on in here?" Merle asked, wiping his face on his tee shirt.

"Did you see him, Merle? Did you see that big snake? I was laying on my bed and he come right under the door and across the floor. He must be six feet long," Quaid said in a quivering voice. "I think he went under the bed." He rocked back and forth, with glazed eyes.

Merle got down on his knees and peered under the bed. "There's no snake in here, Quaid. You must have been dreaming. Now come on down off of that bed."

Quaid slid down the wall and sat on the bed, his body still trembling. "I swear I saw him, Merle. He was real big. He had six or seven rattlers on his tail. I know what he wants. He's the devil, Merle and he's after me."

Merle sat down on the edge of the bed. "Now look, Quaid, how many times do I have to tell you that there are no snakes in this house. I don't know what's bothering you, but you got to get a hold of yourself. You've been acting crazy since we left Texas. What in the hell is going on?"

"If you do something real bad, Merle, will you go to Hell? Will the devil send the snakes up to get you when you die?"

Merle shook his head. "I don't know a lot about Heaven or Hell, Quaid, but I think God is a pretty fair person. If you've done something wrong just tell him you're sorry and he'll probably forgive you. I mean I hear a lot of people finding Jesus and getting a second chance."

"I bet you're right. If I pray real hard, I'll get a second chance. Yeah, that's what I gotta do. I gotta pray and get a second chance, Merle. Where can I find Jesus?"

"I don't know, Quaid. It's something about being a born again Christian. You got to get baptized and stuff. Just pray, Quaid. You'll be fine."

Quaid's face broke into a smile as he fell to his knees next to the bed and folded his hands. "Merle, are we gonna ride on the bus again?"

"Yeah, pretty soon we'll be back on the road. What the heck did you do that was so bad you think you're going to Hell?" Merle asked.

But it was too late to get an answer. Quaid's head was buried in the side of the bed and he was already deep into his prayers.

The Chester County Boys

"What was all that screaming about?" Cletus asked, as Merle entered the rehearsal hall a few minutes later.

"It was just Quaid hollering about those damn snakes again. I wish he'd get over it. Anybody here know what triggered his spell this time?"

Cletus shot Jack a nervous glance, and began rifling through his music. Just then Quaid came into the room. His hair was neatly combed and he had on a clean shirt. "What's everybody staring at?" he said. "Let's play some music."

Carly grinned and patted him on the shoulder. "It's good to have you back, Quaid."

Cletus let out a sigh of relief.

The next several weeks were a whirlwind of rehearsals and meetings. Jim had arranged for Carly to meet with a costume designer and a hairstylist. "You're a real pretty girl," he said, "but anything we can do to make you look better will just enhance your performance. Even the band is sounding pretty good. I think it's time to start our appearances."

Jim gathered them all together for one last briefing. "Okay. Here's the deal. I know you all have been playing in a band for a long time. But this is a little different. You are to follow the program, just as we rehearsed. I don't need any Elvis impersonations," he said, shooting a look at Cletus. "And I don't need anyone trying to be a hot dog. We have a lot at stake. Is everyone clear on this?"

The room was silent. Jim took this as a yes.

CHAPTER SIXTEEN

Carly walked across the stage and looked up at the huge expanse of gold curtain hanging from the rods above her head. Her footsteps echoed through the empty theater as she stared out into the rows and rows of burgundy seats. She took the folded newspaper out of her back pocket and sat down in the middle of the stage. Spreading the paper in front of her, she reread, for the third time, the advertisement in the entertainment section.

Stellar Productions presents live in concert,
CARLY BOONE AND THE CHESTER COUNTY BOYS
Saturday, July 7th and Sunday, July 8th
8PM at the Palace Theater
Tulsa, Oklahoma
Don't miss this opportunity to hear a rising new star
to the country music scene.
Tickets available at the box office or online.

It was hard for her to believe that this was actually happening.

The Chester County Boys

Jim had set up several radio interviews for her and also an appearance on a local television show. She hesitated about the show, but Danny seldom watched television.

Later that afternoon, Jim called Carly into his office. "I'm glad you're here," Jim said as she closed the door. "It's only three days until our opening and I've got some pretty good news. The ticket sales have been brisk and we'll have enough of a crowd to cover all our expenses on this stop and make a few dollars. Our next stop on the circuit will be even better. Looks like you all have got yourselves a few groupies. They've been hanging out around the house.

Carly laughed. "If it's our groupies they must be from the senior citizens homes."

"Don't be so sure of yourself," Cletus said as he came in the door unannounced. "I know we've been around a long time, but we can still turn a few heads. Just because you got top billing and the advertisements didn't even mention our names doesn't mean people don't know who we are."

"Look, Cletus, I wish you would get over it. If you got a problem with how I'm handling things, you can always take off on your own, since you're such a big star and all," Jim said in a disgusted voice. "Spend the next three days getting prepared for the concert. That means no drinking or drugs, plenty of rest, and as many rehearsals as you can fit in. I'll have the house staff fix your meals, so there is no need for you to leave the house. I don't want any mishaps. I'll see you all on Saturday."

Jim picked up his briefcase. "And the next time, keep your ear away from my door and knock before you come into my office."

On the last evening before the show, they made one more run through their numbers and returned to the den. Merle sat in a lounge chair reading the paper as Randy flipped through the television channels.

Quaid stared out the window at the open field behind the house. He could just imagine that there were creatures living in the rocks and crevasses. There could be big rattlesnakes that were waiting for him to walk outside. He began to pray again.

Merle looked up over his paper as Cletus entered the room. "What the hell do you have on, Cletus? Damn if you're not a sight."

Cletus carried a bath towel over his shoulder. He wore a pair of flowered swim trunks, his white hat and cowboy boots.

"I'm gonna take me a dip in that pool. I haven't been in a swimming pool in about twenty-five years. There are some more suits upstairs if anyone wants to join me. We need to have a little fun."

He walked out through the patio doors and jumped into the water. Carly followed a few minutes later. Before the evening was over, everyone was in the pool, except Quaid. He kept his post at the window, watching to see if anything was moving in the expanse of grass.

Carly sat next to Merle on the chaise lounge combing her wet hair. "That really felt good. We really don't spend much time having fun do we?" she asked.

"Not much," Merle replied. "We are a pitiful bunch."

Carly laughed. She paused for a moment. "Have you ever been in love, Merle?"

"Now where did that come from?" he asked.

"Oh, I don't know. I have never heard you talk about anyone special in your life and I was just curious."

"I guess I have been in love, Carly. Or maybe I thought I was a couple of times, but I never had much to offer anyone. A long time ago, there was someone special. Real special, but it didn't work out. How about you?" he asked.

"There was this boy I met in Massachusetts. That was years ago. I was young. What did I know about love? But he sure made my heart beat fast. I really haven't felt the same about anyone since then."

Merle smiled. "Well, darlin, seventeen or seventy, when that feeling hits you it's all the same. How did you get hooked up with Danny?"

"Sheer stupidity, Merle. He was a smooth talker and before I knew it, he had moved into my life and taken over. I truly believe he would have probably killed me if I didn't get away. Let's change the subject. Just talking about him makes me nervous. I just think he is going to show up one of these days."

Cletus was restless after his swim and searched the house for something to drink, finding only a bottle of cooking sherry in the kitchen. He spit the bitter liquid into the sink and cursed. "I'm gonna see if one of those people who work here can run me into town. I need some smokes," he growled.

"I got some extra cigarettes you can have," Merle said.

Cletus grumbled and lay down on the couch, putting his hat over his eyes.

Merle stood up and stretched. "Well, I think me and Randy are going back to the studio and run through some of these songs one more time. I guess Jack must be out there by himself. You want to come with us, Quaid?" Merle asked.

Quaid shook his head and once again continued to stare out the window.

"I don't know what's out there that's so interesting, but by now you should be able to recognize every blade of grass," Merle said as he left the room.

Carly sat on the patio, polishing her toenails. She looked up when she saw the old blue car coming up the driveway. The engine shuddered and a puff of black smoke curled around the muffler. Nadine opened the door and stepped out. She wore a pair of cut-off shorts and a midriff top. Her once red hair was now dyed a brassy blonde. She waved to Carly. "Hi, Carly. I bet I'm the last person you expected to see. Jim said it was all right if I came out to see you. I told him it was kind of an emergency." Carly could only guess what was going on now. She knew it would involve money.

Nadine sat down next to Carly and lit a cigarette. "I've decided to go back to Lubbock. Things just aren't working out too well for me here in Tulsa. I'm not making very good tips at the restaurant and the place I'm living is a real dump. I talked to Lee the other day and she said if I came back to Lubbock I could have my old job back. I'm short on cash. If you could lend me a few bucks, I can get a bus ticket out of here. That car belongs to one of the girls I work with. Gosh, this place is nice. You guys are really living high."

"I know, but not on our money. Jim is paying most of our expenses. I'll have to go to my room and write you a check," Carly said, as Nadine followed her through the patio doors.

Cletus raised his hat up as they entered. "Well, well, look what the cat drug in. What are you doing out here? We aren't giving any free handouts today."

Nadine stuck her tongue out. "Hello to you too, dirt bag. I see you're just as ugly as ever. I'm going to wait outside, Carly. I don't want any of his stink rubbing off on me." She

The Chester County Boys

turned and went back out to the patio, just as the telephone began to ring.

After the third ring, Cletus sat up. "Jesus, Quaid, can you get that? You're sitting right next to it," Cletus said in an irritated voice. "Just pick the damn thing up and say hello."

Quaid slowly picked up the receiver and put it to his ear. "Oh, hello," he said. There was a long silence. "You better talk to Cletus." Quaid held the phone out.

"Give me the damn thing. Who the hell is it?"

"Cletus, it's me, J.B. from the Double L. I had a hell of a time finding you guys. I need to talk to Carly."

"Sorry, she's not here right now, what's going on?"

"Well, I'll tell you and you can tell Carly. Did Carly ever tell you anything about a guy named Danny she used to live with?"

Cletus could feel the sweat beading on his forehead. "Yeah, matter of fact, she did. What about him?"

"Danny's mother and his brother showed up at the Double L the other day. They're looking for Danny. They said that they haven't seen him in over three months. He took his mother's gas card and ran it up big time. He also broke into his brother's business and took money and a car. Danny's mom hired a private detective and seems like he found out that Carly was living in Lubbock. They told the detective that Danny was looking for Carly. They thought maybe she knew where he was. I think when his mom and brother find Danny, they're going to wring his neck. I played dumb, Cletus. I told them people I didn't know where Carly was. I just wanted to call and warn her in case Danny or those people find out she is in Tulsa. How's everything going?" he asked.

"Just fine. Thanks for calling, J.B. I've got to hang up now."

Cletus put the phone down and turned to Quaid. "I have to go tell Jack that Danny is probably still looking for Carly. I don't want him showing up here. I hope you guys did a good job of scaring him off, Quaid."

"He won't show up here, Cletus," Quaid said in a matter of fact voice. "He's dead."

"What? What the hell do you mean he's dead? You and Jack told me that he got away from you two and ran off the night we took him up to the bluff," Cletus said in a stunned voice. "You're lying, Quaid. He ain't dead."

"I ain't supposed to tell you anything. Jack told me not to. He said I would go to Hell if I told anyone. We dropped that man over the cliff. We didn't mean to. It was an accident."

Cletus grabbed the front of Quiad's shirt. "You're telling the truth aren't you. Jesus, I can't believe this. You mean to tell me that you and Jack killed that guy? You dropped him off the cliff! Damn, if this ain't one hell of a mess." Cletus just kept shaking his head.

Quaid began to cry. "We didn't mean to kill him. He just kept fighting us and then he just fell off the cliff. I'm gonna tell Carly and Merle what happened. I want them to know it was an accident. That way I won't go to Hell and I can keep playing my music."

Cletus heard Carly coming down the steps. He put his fingers to his lips. "Not now, Quaid. It's not a good time to tell Carly. You go to your room and lay down and I'll tell her and Merle and that way they won't be mad at you. Now, go on. Just go do whatever you do in there. I'll be there in just a minute and don't come out until I get back." Cletus took Quaid by the shoulders and led him down the hall. "Now you stay in your room and I'll fix everything for you, okay?"

The Chester County Boys

Nadine was sitting on the edge of the pool dangling her feet in the water when Carly came out the patio door. "This sure is a nice pool. I wish I had time to take a swim, but I have to get that car back pretty soon," she said, motioning to the heap of metal that was still smoking.

Carly handed her the check. "Sorry I took so long. I had to do some quick figuring to make sure I had enough money in my account. This is all I can give you." She handed Nadine the check for two-hundred dollars.

"Thanks, Carly. I won't forget everything you did for me."

Nadine folded the check up and put it in her pocket. She stood up and hugged Carly. "By the way do you think you could leave me a couple of tickets at the box office tomorrow night, so I can see your show before I leave?"

Inside the house Cletus was pacing the floor. He had pushed the button on the intercom several times. "Jack if you can hear me, meet me out on the patio, I got something real important to tell you." Rubbing his head, he nervously puffed on a cigarette. Cletus heard the noise of the old car starting up and looked out the window to see Nadine leaving.

"Dammit," he mumbled. He had forgotten she was still here. "What was Nadine doing outside?" he asked Carly as she came in the patio door.

"She was sitting at the pool, why?"

"Nothing. I just wondered," Cletus replied.

The intercom crackled. "What do you want, Cletus? We were right in the middle of a song," Merle said in an agitated voice over the intercom.

"I need to see Jack, right now." Cletus released the button and started toward the door just as Jack rounded the corner. "Come with me," he said taking Jack's arm and leading him into the kitchen.

"Why in the hell didn't you tell me about Danny? You are a lying son of a bitch. Quaid just told me the whole story. I can't believe you guys dropped him off the cliff and now J.B. called and said Danny's family is looking for him. We are in some deep shit. I am sick to my stomach right now."

By this time, Cletus was jumping up and down and trying to light a cigarette.

"Just stop! I didn't tell you because I figured one night you'd get drunk and tell some bimbo in a bar about what happened. I couldn't take that chance. Look how crazy you're acting right now? And as far as Quaid, I thought he would forget about it. I didn't expect him to go even crazier on me," Jack said in an irritated voice. "They ain't found Danny's body yet and I don't think they will. No one has any idea to look down in that canyon. You just keep your mouth shut and play dumb. That shouldn't be too hard to do and everything will be okay."

Cletus put the cigarette out with the heel of his boot. "Oh, so now I'm an accessory to a murder. Maybe Quaid is right, maybe we ought to go tell Merle what happened."

Jack grabbed Cletus by the front of his neck. "Listen to me, little man, don't even think about it or you might find yourself at the bottom of that cliff. I said I'll take care of everything and I will. Now I have to take a walk. You just stay here and make sure that Quaid doesn't get near Merle or Carly."

Cletus gasped and backed up. "Okay, okay, but I don't know why you got to take a walk now."

Jack whirled around, his fists clenched. Cletus hurried down the hall before Jack came after him. Jack picked up a towel from the side of the pool and started walking out toward the open field. He cursed to himself. He had wanted to wait till after the performance on Saturday night to deal with Quaid, but now he couldn't take the chance. Quaid was ready to crack and Jack knew it.

Jack found a sturdy tree branch. He stripped off the leaves and began turning over rocks with the stick; it took him about twenty minutes to find a decent size black snake. Jack wrapped the snake in the towel and headed back toward the house just as the sun was beginning to set. Once in his room, he stuffed the rolled-up towel into his duffel bag.

Quaid was still in his room. He had closed the patio doors and pulled down all the shades. He sat in the middle of his bed, not moving, waiting for Cletus to tell him he could come out. Jack opened the door and called his name. "Quaid, you in here? I'm gonna turn on the lights. Look man I got good news; I just found out that Danny is still alive. We really didn't kill him. He landed on a ledge and someone found him. So now everything is okay. You understand what I'm saying?"

"Yeah, I understand. Danny's okay. That's good, but I still need to tell Carly and Merle. I gotta tell them what happened so they're not mad at me."

Jack slammed his fist on the nightstand. "Dammit, Quaid, why are you being so bullheaded? They don't need to know. I'll tell you what. You stay here and I'll go get you something to eat from the kitchen and we'll talk about how we are going to tell them, if that is really what you want to do."

"Okay. I sure am hungry. Could you bring me two sandwiches?" Quaid asked.

Once he was sure Quaid wasn't going to leave the room, Jack went back to his room and pulled a fifth of whiskey out of the nightstand drawer. He then went to the kitchen and made Quaid two turkey sandwiches and filled a water glass with ice. He wrapped the glass in a napkin and carried the tray to Quaid's room. "Here you go, buddy. Eat up. I know you have to be hungry."

Quaid reached for the glass that Jack had filled with whiskey and took a big drink. As Quaid devoured his sandwiches, Jack continued to fill the glass each time Quaid took a drink. "Come on, old buddy, finish your whiskey and you're gonna feel much better. Quaid closed his eyes and laid his head on the back of the bed. Jack got up and opened the patio door a few inches. "I'll go get Carly and Merle. You finish eating and I'll be back in a few minutes."

Jack reached down and unplugged the bedside lamp. He waited a few minutes until he heard Quaid snoring.

Cletus looked up, as Jack entered the media room. "Uh, is everything okay? How's Quaid?"

"What's wrong with Quaid?" Merle asked. "Is he sick?"

Jack sat down and picked up his guitar. "He said he had a headache and he was going to bed. I checked on him a few minutes ago and he was sleeping. I guess we can just rehearse without him."

The session lasted about two hours. Carly yawned. "I think we should call it a night. We all need to get a good night's sleep. Tomorrow is the big day."

"Yeah, you're right. I'm headed that way right now," Merle said, stretching his arms over his head. Cletus nervously glanced at Jack and left the room with the others.

The Chester County Boys

The house was quiet. Most of the lights had been turned out and the only sound was the pendulum on the grandfather clock in the foyer swinging back and forth. Jack opened his bedroom door and looked up and down the hall. He put the rolled-up towel under his arm and hurried to Quaid's room.

Quaid was still asleep; lying on his side, snoring loudly. The glow of the full moon shone through the French doors. Jack knelt down and crawled across the floor to the side of the bed. Lifting the cover, he unfolded the towel and shook it out.

In a raspy voice, Jack called Quaid's name. Quaid turned over and continued to snore. Jack called his name again. This time Quaid opened his eyes. Jack cupped his hand over his mouth and made his voice quiver. He let out a low moaning sound.

"Who is it? Who's there?" Quaid said in a frightened voice.

"Quaid, I've come to get you. I am the devil. I am here with you under the covers," Jack whispered.

Quaid sat up in the bed, his legs thrashing as he kicked the covers with all his strength. As the blanket fell to the floor, the black snake coiled around and lifted his head. Quaid fell sideways off the bed, hitting his head on the nightstand. He tried to get his balance as he staggered around in the dimly lit room.

"Run out the door, Quaid; run out the door and maybe you can save yourself," Jack whispered as he shook the sheet, making the snake bounce up and down.

Quaid began to whimper. Clawing his way along the wall, he flung open the patio door and staggered out. It was only seconds later that Jack heard the splash of the water.

He grabbed the snake from the bed and threw it out the door. There was no sound coming from the pool. He waited a few minutes more before he wiped off the whiskey bottle and put it on the nightstand. That was all too easy. He had expected he would have to push Quaid into the water. Now his hands were clean.

He opened the door to the hallway and made sure no one was around. He then went back to his room and fell sound asleep.

The next morning, Carly sat at the table eating a piece of toast, while Jack read the paper. She looked up when Merle came into the kitchen. "Quaid is not in his room. Have you seen him this morning?"

Jack rubbed his head and yawned. "Nope. I just got up a few minutes ago. He probably went out to the studio or maybe he took a walk. I don't know."

"No, he always comes into the kitchen first thing. I can't find him anywhere. He couldn't just disappear into thin air," Merle said. "I don't know where else to look. Anybody got any suggestions?" He poured himself a cup of coffee and sat down at the table. "I'm gonna drink this and go search some more."

The back door flew open and Cletus tumbled in. His face was ashen white and perspiration beaded on his forehead. "Jesus! You gotta come outside. Something terrible has happened. Call 911! Call an ambulance! Call somebody!" He turned and ran back out the door, followed by Merle and Carly.

Jack got up from the table. He stretched and slowly poured the rest of his coffee into the sink and walked outside. Merle and Carly had already pulled Quaid's body from the water. Merle knelt down and put his hand on Quaid's cold chest. Quaid's eyes were wide open and his face was a pale shade of gray. A large gaping gash ran across his forehead.

Carly pulled the tablecloth off of the patio table and laid it over him; his left foot with the three missing toes stuck from beneath the cloth. Cletus ran toward the grassy edge of the patio and began to vomit.

It took about ten minutes for the sheriff and his deputy to arrive. The ambulance came a few minutes later. They covered Quaid with a black rubber sheet and put him on the stretcher. Carly and Merle sat at the patio table too stunned to even look away. It was Cletus who rocked back and forth, his arms wrapped around his body. Randy stood back, still in his underwear, softly crying. Only Jack seemed to keep his composure.

Sheriff Phelps opened his notebook and sat down. "Can anybody tell me what happened here? Who was the last one to see him alive?"

Jack spoke up. "I looked in on him last night before I went to the studio and he said he just wanted to sleep because he had a headache."

"Did anybody else see him last night?"

"We all saw him earlier in the evening," Carly answered. "He was sitting in the den with us after dinner."

"Was he acting strange?" Phelps asked

"Quaid always acted strange. He was a little slow, been like that all his life, but lately he's been acting downright weird. He's been talking about snakes and the devil. He kept saying something bad was going on with him," Merle said.

"Well, it looks to me like he got out of bed and wandered out the patio door. He must have fallen into the pool and hit his head," the sheriff surmised. "I'll have to order an autopsy and I want to talk to you each individually."

Merle shook his head. "There is no way Quaid would have gone outside by himself in the middle of the night unless he didn't have any idea what he was doing? Maybe he got confused in the dark and thought he was opening the bathroom door."

Sheriff Phelps wrote a few more things in his notebook and then stuck it in his pocket. "We'll do a full investigation and see what we can come up with. Don't worry, we'll get to the bottom of this. I hear you have a concert tonight. Sorry about your bad luck. I'll keep in touch and tell you when we are going to release the body so that you can make arrangements for a burial." With that he tipped his hat and left.

"This is just awful. Poor Quaid," Carly said shaking her head. "I wonder what possessed him to go outside? I'm so sorry, Merle." She put her arms around his shoulders and hugged him.

Jack had left and gone back into the house with Cletus right behind him. Cletus shut the kitchen door, making sure that Carly and Merle were still outside. "Now, you're gonna tell me what happened last night. Did you kill Quaid? Did you push him in that pool?"

Jack lit a cigarette and leaned against the sink. "No, I did not kill him. Like I told the sheriff, he was asleep when we got done rehearsing, so I just went to bed."

"But you said you were going to take care of Quaid. What did you mean by that?" Cletus asked.

"I had a talk with him. I convinced him that Danny was still alive and he didn't have to worry. That's all. He was in a good mood when I left his room, except for his headache. I sure wasn't planning on killing him."

Cletus sighed. "These last twenty-four hours have been a real bitch. First I find out about Danny and now this. My nerves are shot. I need to get me something to drink even if I have to walk to Tulsa. And you'd better be telling me the truth, Jack." Cletus left the kitchen to find one of the servants and talk them into taking him to the nearest place t buy a bottle of whiskey.

Carly sat outside with Merle, watching as the ambulance pulled away. "It's all my fault, Carly. It's my fault that Quaid is dead. I should have never taken him away from Lubbock. This was just too much for him to handle. And being out here in the desert really scared him. Damn it, why was I so stupid?" Merle said, wiping the tears from his face.

Carly put her hand on his back. "Now, what would he have done if you left him in Lubbock, with no job and no one to look after him? It wasn't your fault, Merle. He just got confused."

"I could have stayed behind with him," Merle said.

"Who knows what went wrong. You were his best friend and he knew it. Please don't blame yourself, Merle. Maybe Quaid had a lot more problems then we knew about."

Merle let out a sob, his whole body began shaking. "I loved that guy. Man I'm going to miss him."

When Jim Colby got the news about Quaid, he was furious. What had ever possessed him to hire a slow-witted fiddle player? He paced back and forth across the studio, his head down as if he were in deep thought. He seemed startled when Merle began to speak. "The concert is only seven hours away and I don't know if any of us feel like performing right now."

"Oh, you're going to perform tonight, you can count on that," Jim retorted. "We have almost a sell out crowd and there's no way I'm canceling. I'm just trying to think of who I can get to fill in for Quaid. I know a couple of really good musicians, but I don't know if they're available. I'm sorry about Quaid, but this isn't the time or the place to make any changes in our schedule. Canceling the first show of a tour is sudden death for all of us. We'll have to figure out what to do about this situation later. He continued to pace back and forth for a moment and then pulled out his cell phone. "I need to make some calls. Start making your final preparations for the show. After tonight's performance you guys can have a week off to get yourself together."

It was a somber afternoon. No one wanted to speak. Merle tried to cope with his grief, while Jack and Cletus worried about the police report. Carly was shocked that Jim was making them perform. They rode in silence to the theater. An hour later, Carly stood trembling as the curtain went up and the huge spotlights circled the stage, finally settling on her face. The audience began to applaud as she stepped forward. She adjusted her headset microphone and crossed her fingers behind her back. She was going to break Jim's rule about following the program.

Her voice cracked. She cleared her throat. "I want to thank you all for coming. I'd like to dedicate our performance tonight to one of our band members who couldn't be with us. His name was Quaid and we miss him. There were only three things Quaid loved: his friend, Merle, his music and riding on the bus. So Quaid, wherever you are, I hope you're listening."

CHAPTER SEVENTEEN

Jim was true to his word and after the show he shuttled everyone back to the house. "Okay, I know I wasn't very sympathetic about Quaid and for that I am sorry. I guess I never really got to know him. I want you to take this time to relax, maybe concentrate a little bit on your music and be ready for what's ahead of you." He looked at Carly. "Are you going to be okay?" She nodded, yes.

The cook prepared dinner for everyone and they ate in silence, each one wondering what the other one was thinking. Cletus put his fork down and pushed his chair out. "I got a good idea. Let's go into Tulsa and get a drink. If we stay here, we're just all going to be miserable. You know Quaid wouldn't want us to be unhappy. Anybody up for it?" Randy and Jack decided to go along, but Merle declined. He wanted to be alone. Carly decided to stay behind and go to bed early.

Cletus pulled his Cadillac up in front of the Rambling Rose Inn and parked. They could hear the music filtering out through the door.

"Looks like this place is jumping," Cletus said as they entered the smoke filled room. Jack disappeared almost immediately and Randy went to the bar. "I'm gonna find me a table. I'll see you guys later," Cletus said.

Cletus ambled across the room, tipping his hat to the ladies and smiling. He was a star. He had to put on a good appearance in case someone recognized him.

Randy ordered a drink and began talking to two girls behind the bar. He stared at their breasts as they bent to retrieve bottles from the beer box. He knew they were doing that intentionally so they would get more tips. It was working for him. He found himself laughing and joking for the first time in weeks. One of the girls asked him a question and pointed to the end of the bar where Jack was sitting all alone. Randy shook his head and they went on talking.

Jack had seen the whole thing. He knew they were talking about him. He would make certain he found out what was going on. He stuck his change in his pocket and got up from the stool. A few minutes later he appeared behind Randy. "Find Cletus! I'm ready to go."

Randy turned around slowly. "Are you talking to me? I'm not your chauffeur. You find him; I'm having a good time." He turned his back to Jack.

Cletus was by no means ready to go either. He was dancing with a redheaded woman in tight pink slacks. He handed his car keys to Jack and said he would find a way home.

When the Rambling Rose closed at three A.M., Randy went home with both of the bartenders and Cletus was in the back room in the arms of the lady in the tight pink pants.

It was almost noon the next day before Randy got home and Cletus was nowhere in sight. As soon as the door opened, Jack came out of his bedroom. "I want to talk to you, Randy. Come out to the patio."

Randy plopped down on the sofa in the den. "Look, Jack. I'm getting tired of you ordering me around. If you have something to say to me, say it and get out of my face."

Jack's voice softened. "Okay, I'm sorry. I guess we've all been on edge. I just wanted to know what those girls were asking you about last night?" He nervously laughed. "I thought maybe you were saving one of them for me."

Randy yawned and laid his head back on the sofa. "No, it was nothing like that. It's just one of the girls thought she recognized you."

"From where?" Jack asked

"Hell, I don't know. She asked me if your name was Robert and I said no."

"What else did she ask you?"

"Cool it, old man. That was all there was to it. You got something to hide, Jack? Come to think of it, none of us know anything about you." Randy sat up. "Maybe I'll make it my business to find out. Yeah, that's what I'll do. I'll hire a detective to check you out."

Jack flew across the floor and grabbed Randy by the front of his shirt. He pulled him up off the couch, just inches away from his face. "Listen to me, Randy. You mind your own business. I find you snooping around about me, you'll be sorry." He let go of Randy's shirt and Randy fell back on the couch.

"Damn, you are crazier then Quaid was. I was just joking around."

He rubbed his hand across his chest. Jack had scared him. Whatever it was that Jack was hiding must be serious. He was through dealing with Jack. He wondered if he should tell Merle, just in case something happened to him. Randy shrugged it off and headed for his bedroom.

Jack paced back and forth across the patio trying to quell his anger. He had controlled it for all these years and now it was clawing its way to the front of his mind. Jack had made himself a promise when he joined the band that he would keep his life to himself. Everyone in the band had always respected his wishes and now it seemed like they were all in his face. He had dealt with Quaid, but Cletus was still a concern. Now, he had to worry that Randy was up to something. He needed to find someway to convince them that everything was okay. That might be a tough one.

Jack waited until the next morning when everyone was home before he approached them. Asking them all to come into the den, he knew they were all wondering what was going on. He started with his prepared speech. "I know I'm not the easiest person in the world to get along with, but I want you all to know I am not a bad guy." Randy rolled his eyes. "Anyway, I have always been a private person mostly because when I was a kid I was really mistreated. It made me turn inward and I've always had a hard time trusting people. This being together all the time has made me real nervous and I lose my temper sometime. So, I'm sorry if I've hurt anyone's feelings. I guess I'm still upset about Quaid." He stopped talking and hung his head. It was quiet in the room for a moment.

Merle stood up and slapped his knees. "Okay, that takes care of that. Let's go eat some breakfast."

Cletus wondered what provoked Jack into making such a pathetic speech. He didn't believe one word of it. He wondered who he was trying to con now.

As they left the room Carly asked Merle, "What was that all about?"

"I haven't got a clue, darlin, and I'm not going to ask. All this togetherness is making everyone nuts. I think I'll find someplace to go fishing today."

By the middle of the week, everyone was not only crabby, but extremely bored. No one had gone near the swimming pool since Quaid died and there was little to do except watch television or sleep. Cletus was the exception. He disappeared every night after dinner and most times did not come home until the early hours of morning.

Merle and Randy lounged in the family room playing a video game when Cletus entered the room. He wore a black satin shirt and white stretch pants tucked into his boots. Merle looked at Randy and grinned.

"I see you got your high-heels on again," Randy said.

"Very funny. You're pretty smart for being stupid. These are standard heels for the expensive boots," Cletus replied.

"What about your hair?" Merle chimed in. "If you plan on swimming you might get arrested for creating an oil slick." Randy and Merle both began to laugh. The sound of voices peeked Jack's curiosity and he opened his door just a crack.

"You guys wouldn't know class if it bit you in the ass. I get compliments on my hair all the time. Besides, I got me a woman and she loves my appearance."

Randy's mouth twitched as he tried not to laugh. "So you got yourself a woman. How many times you been divorced, Cletus? Was it four or five times? You can get a woman, but you sure can't keep them. Where did you find this one?"

"Well, this one is a keeper. She's the hostess down at the Rambling Rose. Her name is Pauline and she is a real looker, if you know what I me." Cletus drew the shape of a woman in the air. "Me and her are keeping steady company. I may even ask her to quit her job and come along on the tour. So what do you think of that?"

"Just make sure you bring along the rock you found her under so she'll have some place to sleep," Merle laughed.

Cletus flipped the catch on his zipper. "Don't you boys worry. I know how to take care of my women. I show them a good time."

"Yeah, I bet when you drop your pants they have the best laugh they've had all day," Randy said. He and Merle roared with laughter.

"You two are shitheads. I'll see you when I see you," Cletus pulled on his belt, tightening the white pants over his groin.

"Hey, look, Merle. I think he put a sock in it."

Randy and Merle rolled with laughter.

Jack quietly closed the door and sat down on the bed. He wondered how much Cletus had told her. It would only be a matter of time before Cletus spilled his guts to this woman.

Cletus pulled his Cadillac onto the highway and turned on the radio. He shifted his position trying to get comfortable. His boots were pinching his feet. Randy and Merle had made him mad. Why did they think he couldn't get a woman? He had lots of women in his time.

Cletus liked women with big breasts and little brains. They were easy to find. His bragging and lies would win them over, but it didn't take long for them to figure him out. His first three marriages lasted less than a year. The fourth lasted almost two years. She was a little slow. She filed for divorce when her finger started turning green from what was supposed to be a five thousand dollar ring. Cletus bragged that he never had to

The Chester County Boys

pay for one divorce. They were all so anxious to get rid of him that they gladly paid to get away.

The next morning Jack left the ranch early. He was once again on a mission. Pauline Page was easy to locate. Just a couple of quick questions at one of the local hangouts produced her address. It seemed like half the men in Tulsa knew where she lived. Jack drove by her apartment and Cletus' Cadillac was still parked in front of her place.

Jack made a u-turn and slowly cruised down the side streets until he spotted a Salvation Army store. He came out of the store twenty minutes later wearing a baggy brown suit and a pair of black rimmed reading glasses. He threw his jeans and shirt into the back seat of his car. He stopped to get himself some breakfast. After he ate, Jack once again drove by Pauline's place and the Cadillac was gone. Parking on a side street, he walked the half block to her apartment and rang the intercom buzzer. A sleepy voice asked who it was.

"Excuse me for bothering you so early in the morning, but I am looking for a Miss Pauline Page," Jack said, using a slight accent.

"That's me," the voice replied.

"I wonder if it would be possible to speak with you. I am Dr. Lightman and I would like to talk to you about a man named Cletus Hurley."

There was silence for a moment and then Jack heard the buzzer, indicating the front door was open.

"Come up. I'm in apartment number five."

Pauline answered the door in a blue silk robe, which she held tightly around her body. Her hair was tussled and she still had on last night's make-up. "What's wrong with Cletus? Is he sick?" she asked. "He just left here a little while ago. Did he have an accident?"

"No, nothing like that. If I could come in for a moment I will explain the situation to you."

Pauline opened the door and pointed toward the flowered couch. She sat opposite him in a lounge chair.

"You see, Miss Page, your friend, Cletus was just recently released from the Bellevue Sanitarium in Enid. I'm not at liberty to give you all the details, but Mr. Hurley suffers from delusional schizophrenia and I am afraid he is not taking his medicine."

Pauline sat up straight. "What in the world are you talking about? What kind of illusions?"

Jack took a small blank notebook and pen from his coat pocket and pretended to read something from it. "Would it be possible, Miss Page, for you to tell me what Mr. Hurley has told you about himself?"

"Well, he said he is the lead singer and guitar player for a real popular band. He told me that he is going on tour soon and cutting an album. He said I could go on the tour with him and that we would have a lot of money to spend. Is he a nut case?"

"I'm really not at liberty to divulge that information. Has he mentioned anything about a man named Jack or perhaps someone named Quaid?"

"No, not at all," Pauline replied. "Who are they?"

"Well, my dear, Mr. Hurley has a lot of strange people living in his head. He is not a musician, but he used to work in a music store. That is before he got sick and was put in the hospital. I'm afraid that when he gets irritated, Mr. Hurley can be quite dangerous, especially when he is not taking his medication. I would suggest that if you continue to see him, you should be careful. He is particularly fond of knives."

The Chester County Boys

Pauline put her hand on her throat. "You don't have to worry about that, Doctor. I don't think I'm planning on seeing im again," she said nervously. "I'll tell him when he calls me today."

"Yes, I think that will probably be best; Cletus will be leaving Tulsa at the end of the week. I plan on having him put back in the hospital as soon as his wife gets here to sign the papers," Jack said.

"His wife! He's nutty as a fruitcake and married to boot. Boy, I can sure pick them. Thanks for coming by, Doctor. Believe me, I don't intend on seeing him anymore. Why do I always end up with the screwy ones?" Her look of horror turned to a smile. "What about you, Doctor? Are you married?" Jack made a hasty exit.

When Jack got back in his car, he threw the glasses out the window and headed for the nearest restaurant to change his clothes. He couldn't believe what an idiot Pauline was. She never once asked how he knew she was seeing Cletus or how he got her address. Of course what could he expect if she was dumb enough to be dating Cletus?

Later in the week when Merle asked Cletus about his hot romance, Cletus replied that she just wasn't his type. He said that she was just a little too low-class for him. He said he had decided that he wouldn't even look twice at another woman unless she was sitting on a bucket of money and had less than a year to live.

Cletus didn't want to talk about it any further. He didn't want to tell Merle that when he went to her apartment to pick her up for a date, a tall, burly man met him at Pauline's door and tossed him down the steps.

CHAPTER EIGHTEEN

It had been two months since Carly and the Chester County Boys started their concert circuit with Stellar Productions. In between shows, Merle flew back to Lubbock with Quaid's ashes. He wanted to go alone.

Merle walked across the bridge that spanned the lake where he and Quaid used to fish every Sunday. He opened the urn and the ashes wafted in the air for a moment and then landed on the water. "Good bye, old friend. I sure don't know what went wrong. I hope you're not mad at me. Have a nice time in heaven. Save me a place." Merle leaned on the rail and stared into the blue-green water. What had really happened to Quaid? He hadn't spoken about snakes since they were kids. Someone must have really scared him and he was going to find out. God help the person who did this to Quaid.

The police report was filed in City Hall in Tulsa, listing Quaid's death as accidental. As far as the law was concerned, the matter was closed. The autopsy report showed that Quaid had an excessive amount of alcohol in his system. They concluded that after consuming the whiskey, he fell, hitting his head on the edge of the pool. Cause of death was listed as accidental drowning.

The Chester County Boys

Merle knew that Quaid loved his whiskey, but he had never seen him take more than one or two drinks. Quaid had asked Merle several times when they were going to ride on the bus again. Staying at the house must have really stressed him more than Merle knew, especially when he became obsessed with snakes.

Carly now had two backup singers and a new fiddle player, named Ray, to take Quaid's place. Jim had purchased an additional bus and hired drivers. Cletus grumbled when he saw Carly's bus. It was plush and spacious, with two bedrooms and a large lounge area. Jim explained the three girls needed the extra space. Jim decided that Tulsa would become their home base. He hired contractors to remodel the rehearsal hall and recording studio at his ranch on the outskirts of town. He planned on keeping Carly close to him. Cletus couldn't understand why they couldn't go on to Nashville first.

It was Carly who was still having trouble dealing with her success and all that had happened to her in the past year. She had never been able to assure herself that her voice was good enough to make a living singing or that it was the right thing to do, but Jim convinced her that she was now a "total package." She not only had a good voice, but she had the looks and stage presence that made her performances work. With the right publicity and appearances, he would make her into a star. For the first time in her life, she had money in the bank.

The band was now back on tour so that they could complete their obligation to Jim and their fans.

Carly sat on a stool looking out into the empty seats of the auditorium, not really sure what town she was in. They had just finished a run through of their performance for the next show.

Jim ran his fingers through his salt and pepper hair and yawned. It had been a long night and he was tired and hungry. The rehearsal had run late because of technical problems and it was after midnight. His footsteps echoed as he walked up the wooden runway leading to the stage. Carly jumped down off the stool and waved to him. "Hi, what are you still doing here? I thought you already left."

"No, I wasn't happy with how the sound equipment was working during rehearsal, so I wanted to come back and check it one more time. Are you hungry? I'm going to get something to eat."

Carly looked at her watch. "I'm not hungry, but I sure could use a good cup of coffee."

In a small, all-night diner, they sat in the booth opposite each other. Jim put the menu down and motioned to the waitress. "A number five, rare, and two coffees. Are you sure you don't want to eat?"

Carly shook her head. "No, coffee is just fine."

"While we're here, Carly, I do have a few things to discuss with you. I was wondering if after the tour is over you would consider moving out to my ranch for awhile? I'm never there and I think it's time you had a home base and get away from the band for a while. When we do the bio for your CD cover, people like to know where you reside. I can't put down that you live on a bus. Besides, I got a real nice recording studio out there and you would have a lot of privacy."

The Chester County Boys

"Gosh, I never thought about it. A bio? Do I have to tell the truth?"

Jim laughed. "Why, do you have a bunch of skeletons in your closet? No, I guess you don't have to tell the truth, but if you get famous, some rag magazine might dig it up and you'll find yourself on the cover of a tabloid, which isn't all bad. At least it means the press is interested in you."

"You never get too friendly with the people you represent, do you, Jim?" She didn't know why she asked that question; she had just blurted it out.

"Not everyone. Sometimes it's hard. You start out thinking you found yourself a star or a good band and sometimes it just doesn't work out. It's easier to tell them that they haven't made the grade when you're not their friend." He smiled at her. "Don't worry. I knew the moment I heard you sing that I could help you become a star."

"I consider you my friend, Jim," Carly said.

Jim grinned, ""Thanks." He wanted to say that he already thought of her as more than a friend. There was something about her that had magnetized him from the first moment he saw her on stage. He planned on getting to know her better and spending more time with her. Up to this point it had almost been impossible.

"How do you think we are doing, Jim?"

"I think you're doing great, but I'm not sure about the band. Even with the new fiddle player and back-up singers, your boys still seem to play the same three cords over and over. This is a tough business. It can change as fast as a raindrop turning to ice before it hits the ground."

"They sat and talked for over an hour; Carly downed three cups of coffee.

"How come you never got married?" Carly asked.

"No woman in her right mind would want a husband that travels forty weeks out of the year. How about you, Carly? Do you have any family?"

She hesitated. "No, none to speak of." She yawned. "Wow, all of a sudden, I'm really sleepy. I better get going." She really didn't want to talk about her past.

Jim stood up and opened his wallet. He laid a twenty on the table. As they left the restaurant, he casually put his arm around her shoulder.

Carly thought to herself it would have been nice to have a father like him.

CHAPTER NINETEEN

Carly sat in the bus with a blanket wrapped around her. Her throat had been sore all week. Cletus came in and threw a letter into her lap.

"Here, this must be fan mail. Jim said it came in the stuff from his post office box in Tulsa."

"You're late," Merle grumbled, glaring at Cletus. "We were supposed to start rehearsing over an hour ago."

Carly picked the letter up, noticing the addresses that were crossed out on the front of the envelope. It looked as if it had been forwarded to several different states. It wasn't until she looked at the return envelope that her hand began to shake.

"Dammit!" she said. "I will never, ever be rid of those people. I knew it was too good to be true."

"Who, darlin?" Merle asked.

Carly held up the letter. "It's from Erlene. She's Danny's sister-in-law." She threw the letter on the chair and stood up.

Cletus put his guitar down. He gulped at the sound of Danny's name. "Well, aren't you gonna open it? It may be important."

"No. Anything those people have to say is of no interest to me. I'm going to lay down for a while."

"Here, let me have it. I'll read it to you," Cletus said reaching for the letter.

Carly picked it up and shoved it into her pocket. "No thanks. I'm perfectly capable of reading my own mail. You guys will have to rehearse without me, my throat hurts too bad to sing."

Cletus couldn't concentrate on his music. Jack leaned over and whispered, "Don't get excited. We'll get the letter after while."

An hour later, they finished their session and the instruments were put away. Cletus knocked lightly on Carly's door. "I'm going over to the café to get me something to eat, Carly. Want me to get you some hot soup? It may help your throat," Cletus asked.

"Sure, that would be great. Let me give you some money."

"It's on me. I'll drop it by the bus."

Cletus loitered outside the bus until Jack came out. "How am I gonna get my hands on that letter, Jack? I got to find out if they found Danny's body. Hell, the law could still be on our tail."

"I already got a plan. Before you take her the soup, mix these two pills in it and then leave the door unlocked on the bus. I'll go over later and get the letter. Will you calm down? It's probably nothing," Jack said, as he handed Cletus the two small white pills.

"What are you giving her, Jack? You better not hurt her."

"It's only mild sleeping tablets. We have to see that letter."

The Chester County Boys

"If you hurt Carly, I swear, Jack Vance, I'll turn your ass into the police, even if it means I got to go to jail, too."

"I'm not going to hurt her. Just do it!"

When Cletus returned with the soup, he carefully open the lid and dropped in the pills. He handed it to Carly and quickly walked away.

Carly took a hot shower and ate the soup along with a dose of cold medication. Suddenly she was exhausted and felt light-headed. It was only eight o'clock, but she turned out the light and fell into her bed.

Jack waited until around ten before he crept into the bus. He stood quietly while his eyes adjusted to the darkness. Looking around the small compartment, he opened the hamper and pulled out the jeans Carly was wearing that evening and put his hand into the pockets.

The letter was not there. Searching around in the dim light, he found it crumbled up in the wastebasket. Jack retrieved the letter and left the bus in haste.

Once outside, he went running in the rain to the second bus parked in the next space. Jack motioned to Cletus, who was looking out the window. Together they jogged across the parking lot to the truck stop restaurant.

Cletus was anxious, but Jack ordered coffee and lit a cigarette. He ruffled the paper and smoothed it across the Formica table in the booth. "Okay, let's see what we got here." He began to read aloud.

Hi Carly,

Long time no see. I guess you're surprised to hear from me. Well, I have some bad news. Danny has been missing for over eight months. If you call that bad news. I say good riddance to bad rubbish. Shirley is crazier than ever worrying about him.

I was wondering if you have heard from him or seen him?

A couple of weeks after you left he came over to Shirley's house and was all pissed off at you. He said he was going to go looking for you. I told him he better not hurt you or I would have him arrested. Anyway, when he left, he stole a gas card from his mom, and a car and some money from Ed. I couldn't stop laughing. Serves them right.

Shirley hired a private detective and he traced Danny as far as Lubbock, but then he lost the trail. So Ed and Shirley went out there, but they didn't have any luck either. What a pair of dumbasses.

Shirley had a life insurance policy on Danny, but she can't do anything with it until she finds out if he is dead or alive. They pestered the police until the captain told them to go home and stay there. Ha. Ha.

I saw your picture in the paper. I'm real proud of you for making it in the music business. I didn't even know you could sing.

Since you had enough nerve to leave Danny, I got enough courage to leave Ed. I'm working as a cosmetic consultant at Wagner's Department Store. I got a couple of boyfriends and I'm having a great time. Ed has the boys and they are driving him crazy. Serves him right for making them so rotten.

Well, I gotta go. If you see Danny, tell him to call his momma.

Maybe someday I can come and see one of your shows or you can send me an autographed CD.

The Chester County Boys

Love Ya, Erlene

Jack folded the letter up and handed it to Cletus. "See, I told you we have nothing to worry about. Nobody would guess that stupid Danny followed us to Tulsa. By now his body has been picked clean by the vultures. So sit back and relax."

"Damn, that is good news. So those cops aren't looking for him. I guess he would be a waste of their time. Whew, I'm glad that's over. Is there anywhere around here that we can get a drink?" Cletus said in a relieved voice.

Carly awoke after a restless night. Her throat was still sore and she could have sworn that she heard someone moving around in the bus late last night. She still felt groggy. She called Jim on his cell phone. "Hi, where are you? I need to talk to you?" she said in a raspy voice.

"I'm in my hotel room. Come on over."

Jim sat on the small settee and waited for Carly. He was nervous. He wondered what was on her mind. When she arrived, she sat down on the chair opposite him.

"What's wrong, Carly? You don't look so good."

Carly rubbed her forehead. "I have a headache, but I'll be okay. I took some cold medicine last night. I didn't realize it was that strong. I have some things I want to tell you. I kept thinking what you said about people looking into my past and I wanted to make sure you knew the truth." She was eager to talk.

"The time I spent in foster homes left me with some pretty mangled memories, so I've tried hard to put them behind me. I try to remember my mother when we had fun together and I try to keep the memory of her voice in my mind. Other than that I would just like to keep my past private. I hope that is okay with you." She paused for a moment. "You know, I was doing okay for myself until I met Danny. I was my own boss and I could do what I wanted. It was really tough to get away from him. Once I started singing again I worried that someday I would look out into the audience and he would be sitting there. It was only recently that I began to relax and then I get this letter yesterday that he is still out there somewhere looking for me. He's a crazy man, Jim. I can't take the chance that he won't come after me. So if you want to tear up my contract right now, I'll understand."

Jim stood up. "Come here, Carly."

"Why?"

"Just come here."

He drew her into his arms and held her. She was surprised, but she instantly buried her head in his shoulder and the tears began to dampen his shirt. Her mother always told her not to cry, that it was a sign of weakness, but this time she didn't care. She had a friend to hold her up.

After a few minutes, he wiped her face and handed her a tissue. "Let me do all the worrying for you. You just concentrate on being a star. Danny Reedy isn't going to get within ten feet of you," Jim said, as he brushed the hair away from her face.

Carly wiped her nose. "Thank you. I feel much better now. How in the heck do people get their lives in such a mess?"

"It's real easy, Carly. It's real easy."

CHAPTER TWENTY

The money from the tour was beginning to change everyone's outlook on their future. Cletus was now sporting expensive red alligator boots and looking at brochures for new Cadillacs. Even Merle had treated himself to some clothes and put money down on a lake-front cabin outside of Tulsa. Jack gave no one any indication what he was doing with his money. He had someone else to worry about now. It was Randy.

On one of their trips back to Tulsa when they were on a break from the tour, Cletus overheard Randy and Merle talking about Quaid. Merle said he was still puzzled why Quaid went outside the night he drowned. Quaid was afraid of the dark and would never leave his room at night alone even if he was drunk. He wondered where Quaid got the whiskey.

Randy told Merle that he was surprised he hadn't heard Quaid scream or make some noise, since his room was right next door. Randy said he was so shocked when Quaid died, that he guessed he didn't remember everything that was going on that night. Randy said that maybe they should try to find out where he got the whiskey from.

Cletus immediately found Jack and told him what he had heard. Jack was silent for a moment. "Okay, I think I know what we have to do. I'm gonna need your help on this one, Cletus."

"No! No! Not me, I'm not getting involved in another one of your crazy schemes."

"Why do you think Randy played with our band, Cletus? He liked the idea of sitting up on that platform playing the drums. It made him look good. He was always winking at the girls and making sure he didn't go home alone at night. It was no secret that he didn't like any of us, especially you. You were too stupid to know that he was always making fun of you while you were on stage. He would make faces or gestures.
That's what made the audience laugh. He was making a fool out you. I have never liked him."

"How come you never told me this before?" Cletus asked.

"Cause, I never liked you any better than I like him. Since Quaid died, Randy spends a lot of time with Merle. I guess we can just sit around and wait till they figure out something about Danny, too."

Cletus groaned. "He is just a stupid kid. He ain't gonna figure out anything. You ain't planning on killing him, are you, Jack?"

"Course not. I've never killed anyone and I sure don't intend to kill Randy. I just want him gone. I got a couple of ideas that should make it real simple. He leaned forward and began telling Cletus his plan.

"Damn, Jack. Where do you come up with these ideas?" Cletus asked.

He wanted to run. Cletus didn't want to get involved in anymore of Jack's schemes. Jack always reminded Cletus that Nashville would not become a reality unless everything went smooth. Cletus had no choice but to listen to Jack and go along with his crazy plan. He knew that they were on thin ice with Jim Colby, but every show brought them one step closer to the Opry. It was hard to give it all up now.

It was the subtle hints that began to annoy Randy, like bits of conversations he overheard between Cletus and Jack. They would usually stop talking when he came into the room, which was all part of the plan to annoy Randy. Randy was beginning to think that there were things going on he didn't know about.

When Jack decided that Randy was getting a little edgy, he put another part of the plan into action. Jack took a deposit slip from his checkbook and filled it out. He purposely dropped it on the floor when he saw Randy coming in the door. Randy walked past it and then stopped and picked it up. He looked at it for a moment, a frown covering his face. Jack came around the corner and grabbed it out of his hand, pretending to be annoyed. When Randy questioned the large amount of the deposit, Jack said it was for a week's pay. Randy was livid. He said he didn't make near that much. Jack said he guessed that is why Jim had told everyone not to discuss their wages. Randy said he had never had that conversation with Jim and just assumed they were all making the same thing.

When Randy continued to badger Cletus about what he was getting every week, Cletus told him he was drawing the same as Jack. The plan was moving forward.

Everything came to a head a few days after they went back on the road. They had a circuit date in Waco. Making sure that Randy could hear them talking, Cletus and Jack stood outside below the bus window.

Jack was saying it was a shame that Jim was going to cut Randy from the band before the end of the tour. Cletus agreed with him. Randy threw open the door of the bus and went outside. Jack had already slipped out of sight and Cletus said he didn't know what Randy was talking about. Randy got into his car and sped down the road toward Waco. He spent the rest of the morning downing shots. Around two o'clock, he left the bar and went to Jim's hotel.

An hour later, Jim called Merle. "I don't know what got into him," Jim said. "Randy came busting into my room and got in my face and said he wasn't working for peanuts any more. He yelled that he wasn't going to wait around until I gave him the boot. Before I could open my mouth, he said he quit and if I wanted to sue him for breaking his contract, I could go right ahead. Do you have any idea what set him off?" Merle said he had no idea what set him off.

After his conversation with Jim, Merle found Cletus and told him they needed to talk. Sitting in the restaurant, Merle asked Cletus if he knew what was going on with Randy. Cletus said that Randy was doing a lot of drugs lately and acting a little crazy. That is all he knew.

When Randy returned from Jim's office, he bounded up the steps of the bus and jerked open the door. It hit the wall with a bang. Jack was lying on the couch with his hat over his face. "Okay, old man, you got your wish. I quit the band. I'm leaving." He pulled his duffel bag from the overhead compartment and began packing his clothes. "You seen my leather jacket? I can't find it."

Jack did not answer. He was grinning under his hat.

"Look, I know you aren't sleeping. When I get to where ever the hell I'm going, I'll call and tell you so you can send the rest of my stuff. Did you hear me old man?"

The Chester County Boys

Jack could hear Randy cussing and fuming as he packed his things in his bag. The phone rang. Jack reached over and picked it up.

"Jack, this is Jim. Is Randy there?"

"No," Jack replied.

"Well, if you see Randy, tell him we need to talk. I'm going to be here until five. Tell him if he gets his ass back to the hotel, I'll forget about what he said today. If he is not here by then, he is officially fired. You got all that?"

"Yeah," Jack replied and hung up.

"Was that for me?" Randy asked.

"Nope, wrong number."

Randy raced down the highway at a break-neck speed. He was still seething inside, yet as each mile passed, he became more and more anxious. Maybe he had made a mistake quitting the band. He should have talked to Merle before he left. Merle would have been straight with him. Besides, even if they were making more money than him, the checks he was getting weekly were more than he was making in a month at the Double L. Living in the bus was keeping his expenses really low.

What if they did get a recording deal? Damn, he was mad at himself. He was even madder at Jack. He should have never let him get under his skin. Randy knew that Jack liked to stir up trouble and then pretend he was an innocent bystander. Somehow he would get even with him.

Randy made a u-turn in the grassy median and headed back towards Waco. It was just a little after six. Jim was probably still at the hotel. The show didn't start until nine. The streets were congested with late-afternoon traffic, but Randy was calm now.

So, he had made a mistake. He would apologize to Jim and everything would be okay. It was almost seven when he finally got to Jim's hotel. Jim wasn't in his room. The desk clerk let the phone ring ten times. When Randy insisted, the clerk sent a bellman to the room to knock on the door. He confirmed that he was not in. Randy glanced at his watch. He had wasted another half-hour. It was seven-thirty. He would go to the auditorium and wait for Jim.

Once back in his car, Randy turned left. After going several miles he realized he was going the wrong way. Turning up a side street, he looked in his rearview mirror to see a flashing blue light behind him.

The officer gave Randy a speeding ticket and directions. It was now close to eight-thirty.

It was Carly who interceded when the security guard at the door refused to let him in. "Randy! What in the world did you do? Why in the hell did you quit the band?"

Randy shrugged. "I dunno, bad day, I guess. I'm okay now. Where's Jim? I need to apologize to him."

"Oh, Randy, I'm so sorry. Jim has already terminated your contract." She motioned toward the stage. "He waited until almost seven before he called in a temporary replacement for you. He was livid. He told me he might even sue you for breach of contract."

Randy was stunned. How could that be possible?

"What went wrong, Randy? I thought things were going good. Gosh, we only have four shows left and then we would have all been together back in Tulsa."

"It was Jack," Randy said. "He told me that Jim was planning on letting me go after the tour ended and he also told

The Chester County Boys

me that the rest of the band was making about twice what I was. Hell, Carly, that really upset me, so I quit."

"Randy those things are the farthest from the truth. Everyone in the band is making the same amount of money. Jim liked you. He had no intention of letting you go. I am so sorry you quit without at least talking to me first."

Randy clenched his fists. "I have to go." He bolted toward the stage door and kicked it open. Leaning over the metal railing, he began to wretch and gag. A few minutes later he stood up, and wiped his mouth on his sleeve. Walking toward his car, the tears welled up in his eyes. "You are going to be so sorry for what you did to me, Jack Vance. Someway, somehow, I'm gonna get even with you."

CHAPTER TWENTY-ONE

"Well, well, if it isn't one of the big time stars," Lee said as Randy ambled up to the bar in the Double L. "What are you doing here? I thought you were still on tour?"

"I'm thirsty. I just came in for a beer. What's been going on around here?"

"Why do you care? You're in the big time now," Lee replied.

Randy shrugged. "I'm just making small talk. You don't have to get mad about it."

"If you must know, I'm doing good. I finally got paid my insurance money from the fire. The police still think it was arson." She pointed toward the other side of the bar. Looks different in here, doesn't it? I took out that crummy stage and put in an all-new karaoke sound system. Best thing I ever did. It's cheap, doesn't talk back and when I'm tired of listening to it, I can just turn it off. I got some guy who comes in a couple of times a week and teaches line dancing and the place is packed. By the way, I heard about Quaid. That's a damn shame. He was a nice old guy. Now tell me what's really going on? Why are you here?"

"I told you I just stopped in to have a drink." He hesitated for a moment. "You don't need an extra bartender do you?" Randy asked.

Lee snickered and slapped her knee. "Damn, I knew you were down on your luck. If you want to work for two bucks an hour and tips, you can have a job. Now, what happened, you get fired?"

"Naw, I quit. It just wasn't my thing. I really don't want to talk about it," Randy replied.

Lee shrugged. "Easy come, easy go. You can start tonight if you want to. Be here at eight." She got down from the stool and headed toward her office with a smile on her face. She never again asked him about the band, although she was curious. Lee would never let on that she was still angry for them leaving her. Right now, she felt like she had finally gotten a little piece of revenge.

That afternoon, Randy rented a room in the motel across the street from the Double L and threw his duffel bag on the bed. He was back where he started, but even in worse condition. Two bucks an hour, that was sick. He was making nine hundred dollars a week with the band. This was only temporary. He would be back on top in no time. Why had he been so foolish with his money. Randy sat up and opened his wallet. He had about six-hundred dollars left from his last check. He had to be careful until he came up with a plan. It happened sooner than he expected.

At the end of his first shift as bartender at the Double L, Randy put the beer bottles in the trash bin and washed out all of the glasses. As he reached to put them back on the shelf, someone covered his eyes with their hands. "Guess who?" she giggled.

Randy took her hands down and turned around. "Oh, hi, Nadine."

She put her arms around him and kissed his cheek.

Nadine wore a tight white tee shirt and a short denim skirt, which crept up her thighs as she reached to kiss him.

"I can't believe you're back. Tell me what happened. I want to know everything," she said. "Why in the world are you working in this dump again?"

"Not now, Nadine. I have to get the bar cleaned up. Lee is over there giving me dirty looks. You better get your station cleaned up."

Randy reached for his tip jar, which held only a few dollars and some change. He cursed under his breath.

After J.B. locked the door, Randy poured himself a glass of Jack Daniels and drank it in one gulp. He screwed up his face, and poured another one. "I see you watching me, J.B. Don't worry, I'll pay for my drinks."

Nadine wiped the last of the tables off and brought her tray of empty bottles to the bar. "It was a good night," she said as she pulled wadded up bills from her apron pocket and went behind the bar.

"Yeah, I guess I would have had a good night too, if I dressed like you," Randy said in a sarcastic voice.

Nadine laughed out loud. "Silly, if you dressed like me, you would probably get more than tips." She lit a cigarette and poured herself a glass of beer. A few minutes later she slid off the bar stool and ambled over to the jukebox. As the music began to play she motioned to Randy. "Come dance with me. We have the whole floor to ourselves."

"Hell, are you kidding? My feet are so tired I can't even feel them. I'm going to bed."

The Chester County Boys

Nadine stood in the middle of the empty floor swaying back and forth as the neon lights from the jukebox made patterns on her face. "Come on, just one dance, it will make you feel better." She kicked off her shoes and walked across the floor. Taking his hand, she pulled Randy out onto the floor.

Nadine didn't dance with him. She attached herself to his body. Her breasts pushed into his chest as she wrapped her arms around his neck. Nadine moved slowly to the music, her leg rubbing on his inner thigh. Randy could feel the beads of sweat forming on his upper lip.

Nadine's breath moved the small hairs on his neck, sending a quiver down his back. Randy groaned. "Why don't we continue this dance over at my place?"

She reached up and kissed him, her tongue playing on his upper lip. She giggled as he took her arm and led her to his car. "Why can't we just walk across the road? Just leave your car here."

"Honey, right now, walking is too painful."

They made love most of the night. Nadine was relentless. Randy finally pushed her off of his body and said, "Enough! Lord, girl, give me a break."

Nadine rolled over and sighed. "That was real good, Randy. I needed that. It's been too long."

He watched her as she sauntered across the floor to the bathroom. "I'm gonna shower. Care to join me?" she said grinning.

"Hell, why not?" Randy bounded into the bathroom and caught her in his arms just as the water ran over them.

They lay in bed, wrapped in the worn sheets of the motel, their damp bodies spent from the long night. Nadine yawned. "Randy, why didn't you ever hit on me when I worked at the Double L? And how about all that time we spent together on the bus, you must have known I was interested in you. Was it Carly? Were you and her having a thing?"

"No. I tried with Carly, but she wasn't interested. And you, you were interested in everybody, Nadine. Besides Merle told me you were messing with a guy name Joel and he was bad news. I didn't need any trouble. You were a real pain in the ass when you were on the bus. You must have known that."

"I messed that one up real good. I had a free ride and I screwed it up. As far as Joel, yeah, he was a real loser. He's in prison now. I don't expect he'll be out till he is a really old man. I'm going to sleep now. Goodnight."

Randy watched her as she turned on her side and rolled up in a fetal position. She was so childlike.

Over the next few weeks they spent every night together. Randy finally told Nadine what happened with the band. She told him how sorry she was, and he could tell she was sincere. Randy bought the trade paper every week and looked at the ads. He needed to get back in the music business. Bartending was not his forte, even though a lot of the women coming into the bar enjoyed his banter and quick hands as he drummed out songs on the glasses with a knife. His tip jar was getting fuller every night. The anger had never gone away and he still felt that someday he would get even. And then there it was, one little paragraph on the back page of the paper that set his plan in motion.

Nadine had spread the newspaper out on the bed and opened the pizza box. Randy flipped on the television and sat down. Nadine pulled a slice of pizza out of the box, the sauce dripping down on the paper. As she wiped the spill with a napkin, her eye caught an article in the paper.

"Oh my God!" Nadine exclaimed. "Look here, Randy. Read this."

Randy was engrossed in the television program. "You read it to me."

Nadine began to read.

"*Tulsa police have confirmed that the decomposed body found at the bottom of Knobs Bluff in Barrie Canyon Park was that of Daniel Reedy of Sweetwater, Texas.*

According to the police report, two hikers were repelling down the canyon wall when they spotted a wallet in the fissure of a large boulder. They turned it into the police who sent a crew out to the location. On further inspection, human remains were found three hundred feet below in the canyon floor.

The coroner's initial findings indicate that the remains have been there for at least nine months to a year. The death has been deemed a homicide since the presence of duct tape was on the wrists of the skeletal remains.

Anyone having information that will assist in the circumstances surrounding this death, please contact the Tulsa Police Department."

Randy rolled over and leaned on his elbow. "So, what are you telling me? What's all this about?"

"Randy, you remember Carly talking about him. Danny Reedy was Carly's ex-boyfriend. She told me that she took off and she was afraid he was going to come after her. He used to bounce her around and she said he had a violent temper. He pissed a lot of people off."

"So, somebody got tired of him and pushed him off a cliff. What does that have to do with you and me? I'm just glad for Carly."

"I know who killed him," Nadine said in a soft voice.

"What?" Randy sat up and put on his underwear. "You're freaking me out, Nadine. Start over."

Nadine began to whimper. "I have never told anyone, Randy. You have to promise me that you won't say a word. Do you promise?"

"Yeah, sure, I promise. Now tell me."

Nadine recounted the day she went out to the ranch in Tulsa to borrow money from Carly. She told him about overhearing the conversation between Cletus and Quaid.

"I couldn't believe my ears when Quaid told Cletus that he and Jack had dropped Danny over the cliff. I thought Quaid was just making up some crazy story. Cletus seemed pretty upset, so I figured he knew something about Danny's disappearance. I thought about going to the police, but it would have been my word against his. He probably had an alibi and they would just think I was trying to make trouble for him because he kicked me out of the house. I didn't even know where or when it all happened. I really hate Cletus. I would have loved to get him in trouble. I even started to tell Carly what I heard, but I wasn't sure she would believe me either, so I decided to just let it go."

Randy reached over and took the paper. He reread the article. "Do you know what this means, Nadine? Now I know why Quaid was acting so crazy. I guess Jack was afraid he was going to tell Merle what happened, so Jack tormented him and then pushed him in the pool. That bastard. He had no right to kill Quaid."

Nadine looked puzzled. "Oh, my gosh, poor Quaid. I bet Cletus had something to do with that, too."

Randy stood looking out the motel window for a few minutes. "I'm going to Tulsa. If you want to come along, that's fine. Go pack your clothes and meet me back here in an hour." Nadine began to say something, but Randy stopped her. "You're either with me or not? What will it be?"

"I'm with you, Randy."

After Nadine was dressed, she stopped at the door. "What about Lee? Should I tell her that we're leaving?"

"Screw, Lee. Just go pack."

Once on the road, a breathless Randy filled Nadine in on his plan. He started by telling her how much he hated Jack and Cletus for what they did to him. They were going to pay. They were going to pay big time.

The tour was on break for a week before their last two shows and then on to Nashville at the Grand Ole Opry. Jim planned on making some changes. Carly and the band were back in Tulsa, staying at Jim's ranch. That is where Randy was headed.

CHAPTER TWENTY-TWO

Cletus pushed open the door to the studio and stopped in his tracks. Carly was talking to two police officers and a man in a brown suit. He shut the door quietly and retreated to the house. What were they doing out here? He once again felt the queasiness in the pit of his stomach. He hurried down the hallway to Jack's bedroom. "Jack, Jack, are you in there?"

Jack opened the door and glared at Cletus. "What? What's your problem now?"

"Carly is talking to some cops. What do you think they want?"

Jack sat back down on the bed and pitched a newspaper at Cletus. "It's probably about this," he said pointing to the article on the back page.

Cletus nervously picked it up and began to read. After a few moments he let out a groan. "I knew it. Dammit, why now, when things are going so good? Just one more week and we would be in Nashville. I'm just gonna lay down and die."

"Will you just cool it, Cletus? Of course, those guys have to talk to Carly. She was Danny's ex-girlfriend. That's all it's about. There is absolutely no connection between Danny and us. No evidence whatsoever. No one saw us and they don't have a motive to connect us to Danny, and besides, we have an iron-clad alibi. Go out to the studio and act normal. I'm warning you, Cletus, you better not say a word. You know you could disappear, too."

By the time Cletus got up enough nerve to go into the studio, the police had already left. Carly sat on the couch, tears running down her face. Her hands were trembling.

"Hey, what's the matter, Carly? Why the tears?" He tried to remain calm, but his insides were shaking.

"It's an old wound that just got reopened. Or maybe it has never healed. Someone killed Danny, and the police were here asking me a couple of questions. It's so strange. They think he followed me to Tulsa because he checked into a motel real close to the stadium the same night we opened the show. No one remembers seeing him at the arena, but the clerk at the motel said he never came back for his things so he just pitched them in the trash." No mention was made of the car. "I don't know why I'm crying. I guess I really never wanted him dead, I just wanted to be left alone."

"Uh, did they say if they had any leads?"

She shook her head. "No. They said it's a cold trail and I was of no help to them. They got my name from Shirley Reedy. I'm sure she probably thinks I had something to do with his death."

"So, are they planning on coming back?"

"Why are you asking me all these questions, Cletus? Do you know something about what happened to him?"

"No! What the hell would I know? I was just concerned for you." He pretended to be looking over some sheets of music, all the while waiting for her to give him more information. "You know, I don't want them getting you all upset when we have just a couple more shows to do." He awkwardly patted her on the shoulder. "Well, you take care of yourself, I gotta go."

Cletus went to his room and locked the door. He was going to have to keep an eye out for Jack at all times. He pulled a fifth of whiskey out of the nightstand drawer and lay down on the bed. By the time he fell asleep, the bottle was empty.

Randy and Nadine arrived in Tulsa late on Monday. They decided to settle in before beginning their plan. After a couple of hours of driving around, they found a trailer park about ten miles from the ranch that had a vacancy. Randy paid the owner a week's rent in advance for a one bedroom trailer that was smaller than the bus. It was old, smelly and sparsely furnished. Randy ducked his head as he entered the trailer. "Wow, this place is a mess. It'll have to do until we start collecting some cash from our benefactors."

"I'm sick of living in these kinds of places, Randy. hope we get some money soon," Nadine said.

The next morning Randy called the ranch. He spoke to Jack and told him that he if knew what was good for him, Jack better meet them at the trailer. Jack declined saying he would rather meet somewhere private. He suggested the old gristmill about four miles from the house.

Jack never mentioned the telephone call to Cletus. Jack was surprised when he heard from Randy, but he really wasn't worried. He had no idea what he wanted, but whatever it was, he could handle it.

Jack arrived first and waited until he saw the dust kicking up from the road. When he saw Nadine in the car, he

The Chester County Boys

knew Randy was up to no good. He leaned against his car and lit a cigarette. Nadine turned her head and would not look at him.

Once Randy began relating Nadine's story about what she overheard at the ranch, Jack could feel the rage boiling inside of him. Randy said he knew that Jack and Cletus were indeed responsible for Danny's and Quaid's deaths.

"You're lying," Jack said calmly. "You're trying to bluff me into admitting something that never happened."

"Well, maybe I'll go find Merle and tell him what really happened to his old pal, Quaid. He might find it interesting," Randy said.

Jack glared at Nadine. He hated her. "All right. Let's just suppose I do know something about Danny's death and I'm not saying I do. What do you want from me? If it's blackmail, you aren't going to get a whole hell of a lot. If it's getting back in the band, you know I have no control over that."

Randy began to laugh. "That's real funny, Jack. Why in the hell would I want back in the band, when I can make money an easier way? Let's talk percentages. Don't try to tell me that you guys aren't going for the record deal with Carly. I know differently."

Jack clenched and unclenched his fists. "So, it's blackmail, plain and simple you're after. I have no idea what happened to Danny and Quaid's death was an accident," Jack said, flipping the cigarette onto the ground and grinding it out with his boot.

"Doesn't matter," Randy replied. "Either way, I'm sure the police would reopen the cases. Course I could tell Merle and Jim, but then you won't make any money and neither will me and Nadine. So I'd rather keep it a business deal between us. I'm thinking about a thousand a week to start."

Jack threw his head back and laughed. "Screw you, Randy, I'm not giving you a damn dime. You better get some proof before you go accusing people of murder. I could have you arrested for attempted blackmail and harassment. You're telling me that you believe Nadine?" He pointed his finger at her through the open car window. "You, my little lady, are sadly mistaken. I don't know what you thought you heard, if you even heard anything, but these are some serious charges."

Once again Jack was in control. Nadine stuttered. "I know what I heard. Quaid said that you killed Danny."

Jack began to laugh. "Man, how long did it take the two of you to think this one up? Quaid didn't have the sense he was born with. Who would ever believe him? I gotta go. I don't have time for this crap."

Randy seemed stunned at Jack's response. He expected it to be much easier than this. "Okay, man, you're asking for it. Now I want two thousand dollars. And if you think I'm bluffing, just try me." He whirled around and headed for his car with Nadine following right behind him.

Jack knew that Randy was nervous. Randy didn't have a criminal mind and it would be hard for him to pull this off unless he knew for sure that Jack was guilty.

The next day, Jack called Randy. He wanted to talk to him again. They made plans to meet the following night at the trailer. Jack said he would be there at midnight.

Randy stuck his cell phone in his pocket and flopped down on the bed next to Nadine. "See, I told you he would come through. He knows we have him by the gonads. I'm

The Chester County Boys

thinking to avoid the hassle we'll just have them put the money in a locker at the bus station each week and then we can pick it up whenever we want. Now, let see, what shall we buy first?"

"Do you know what I want, Randy?" Nadine said. "I want a real leather purse; one that smells like leather and has a wallet to match. I've never had a real leather purse."

"Babe, when I get through with Jack and Cletus, you can have a dozen leather purses."

"But, I'm scared of Jack. He has such cold eyes and if he killed Danny and Quaid, what makes you think he won't kill us too?" Nadine said.

"Hey, babe, don't worry. If he wasn't gonna go along with me, he wouldn't be coming out here. Jack knows we got the goods on him. He just likes to intimidate people."

On Thursday night, Jack left the house through his bedroom window around nine o'clock. He was gone for about an hour. No one saw him leave and when he returned he slipped quietly through the same window. It was only after he got back that he called Cletus to his room and told him what was going on. Cletus, clad only in blue boxer shorts, began crying and shaking and telling Jack that he needed to pee. Jack pushed him across the room and told him to go put some clothes on and to stay out of sight until he came for him.

Cletus got dressed. He sat in his room for awhile and then went out on the patio. Carly was sitting in a lounge chair listening to music on her headset.

"Guess I'll turn in. Don't stay up too late. You need to get your beauty rest." He faked a smile and went back to his room. Carly had no idea what he had said.

At eleven-thirty, Jack tapped on his window and helped Cletus climb out. They were on their way to the trailer park.

Cletus parked the car in an obscure location, and they walked in silence to the trailer. Jack looked up and down the narrow road before knocking on the door. Randy yelled for them to come in. Nadine was lying on the bed, pretending to be asleep and Randy was slumped in a chair watching television.

"Welcome, Gents," Randy said, yawning. "Why did you have to make it so late? Let's get down to business."

Cletus looked around the room. "Is this the best you could do? This place is a dump. Why are you trying to cause us trouble, Randy? What did we ever do to you?"

Randy laughed. "Don't act like you don't know, Cletus. Man, you screwed up big time when you hooked up with Jack. Besides, this place is only temporary. Don't worry, by next week I plan on having a much better place."

Jack pulled a folded paper out of his jacket pocket and handed it to Randy. "This is my offer. Take it or leave it."

Randy looked over the paper and a smile crossed his lips. "This sounds good, Jack. Yeah, this sounds real good. So when is payday?"

"I'll get it to you on Monday," Jack shivered. "It's cold in here. Can I turn on the heat?" Before Randy could answer him he got up and went over the space heater that was mounted on the wall. With his back to Randy, he fiddled with the dial, pretending to ignite the pilot light; he lit a match and then blew it out. Turning around, he slid the paper he had given to Randy off of the table and put it in his pocket. "Well, I guess that takes care of everything. We have to get back to the ranch."

The Chester County Boys

Randy stood up, and put his arm around Jack. "Now, see Jack, that didn't hurt so bad. I knew you would come to your senses."

Jack wanted to punch him in the face. Instead, he smiled and he and Cletus left.

Making sure there was no one around, the two hurried along the gravel path, staying in the shadows of the dim overhead lights. It wasn't until they were in the car that Cletus let loose on Jack. He wanted to know just what Jack had promised to give Randy and why he hadn't discussed it with him. "Why did you bring me all the ways out here if you were just gonna give in to him? Hell, I could have stayed at the ranch."

"It's over and done with, Cletus. I told you not to worry. I got some money put aside and I'll take care of paying them. You won't have to chip in at all. Randy settled for peanuts. He could have gotten a lot more out of me. Desperate men make desperate choices," he said laughing. Something he rarely did. "I just wanted you along to make sure that Randy didn't try to jump me or something."

Cletus wasn't relieved. It seemed all too simple. It wasn't like Jack to give into someone's demands. Cletus had seen him go off on stagehands for bringing him the wrong kind of sandwich. Why would he give into Randy's blackmail? Something smelled fishy.

Monday came and Cletus could not wait to ask Jack if he had paid Randy.

"It's none of your business. I told you I would take care of it," he said. "It's over and done with."

Now, Cletus knew something was going on. He had to find out. His life was on the line and he wasn't going to settle for Jack acting like it was no big deal. The next morning, he burst into Jack's room. "All right! Come clean. What did you do? What am I an accessory to now?"

Jack snickered. "I didn't do a thing. Here, read this."

He reached into his nightstand drawer and pulled out Sunday's paper. He moistened his finger and turned the pages until he found what he was looking for. He folded the paper in half and handed it to Cletus.

Cletus sat down and began looking at the page. His eyes settled on an article in the second column. His lips moved as he read the print. "Oh, shit! Not again. Damn, you are one crazy son of a bitch." He threw the paper down and bolted from the room.

Police are still investigating the gas explosion at the Starlight Motor Home Park.

A trailer exploded at twelve a.m. on Thursday night. According to the occupants of the mobile home that live a few hundred feet away, they were awakened by a loud blast. By the time they exited their own trailer, they were met by intense heat and gas fumes from the mobile home across the road and it was engulfed in flames.

The owner of the Starlight Trailer Park said that the couple that had rented the mobile home had only occupied it for several days. Police are still combing the wreckage to make positive identification of the man and woman killed.

When Jack slipped away earlier in the evening on Thursday, he once again was on a hunt. This time he wasn't looking for snakes. He was looking for an empty bird's nest.

The Chester County Boys

It took him a while, but once he found it, he drove to the trailer park. Quietly slipping around the back of the trailer, he found what he was looking for. There was a small flue pipe extending out of the back of the trailer.

Jack knew that these old trailers were heated by space heaters, fueled by propane tanks. The odorless gas was hard to detect. Jack shoved the bird's nest into the pipe and packed twigs and dead grass around it.

Later that night when he pretended to turn on the space heater, neither Randy nor Cletus saw him blow out the pilot light. That's all it took.

Jack knew Randy always smoked a cigarette before he went to bed. Carly complained every night when he smoked on the bus. She said she didn't like the smell of smoke, plus she was afraid he was going to fall asleep and burn the bus up.

Randy was tired on Thursday night. After Jack and Cletus left, he laid down in bed and lit his cigarette. Jack was not someone you blackmailed.

After finding out about Randy and Nadine, Cletus developed a case of colitis that kept him in bed for three days. His stomach ached and the only way he could get some sleep was to drink until he passed out.

His nerves were shot. He knew he was next on Jack's list. After all, he knew everything. He was sure Jack wanted to kill him.

Cletus' imagination ran wild as he tried to figure out how he would meet his fate. All he ever wanted was to go to the Grand Ole Opry and perform. Now his dream was almost in view, but Jack was blurring his vision. Maybe he needed a plan of his own. He decided to start by writing everything down in a letter to Merle. He hid it under the felt lining in his guitar case.

If Jack made his move, he would at least have a little insurance. Jack solemnly told Carly and Merle about the explosion when they woke up on Sunday morning. Carly was almost hysterical. She clung to Merle. "This is insane. It can't be happening again. I had no idea that Randy and Nadine were even in Tulsa. I think I just want to go far away from this place." She broke down and sobbed. Her mother was right. Her singing had done nothing but cause bad luck for everyone.

Jim Colby decided to put the tour on hold even though there were only two shows left. He knew Carly was in no frame of mind to perform. This kind of publicity was driving him crazy. He had never had such bad luck with all the tours he produced. If it weren't for the contracts he had signed in the two remaining cities, he would shut the whole thing down.

That kind of publicity would really be bad for him, plus he would have to pay back a whole lot of money for ticket sales. He had to rethink his strategy.

CHAPTER TWENTY-THREE

Captain Bob Gehring sat at his desk and tapped his pencil on the folder in front of him. A knock on the door interrupted his thoughts. "Come on in, it's open," he said.

Mike Rotaglia walked to the edge of the desk and extended his hand. Captain Gehring motioned for him to take a seat. "Good to meet you, Mike, I've heard a lot about you."

Mike wasn't sure that was good or bad. He had only been on the Tulsa force for six months. What could Captain Gehring possibly know about him?

Bob Gehring picked up a rolled up newspaper and smacked it on the window behind him. "Damn pigeons, I hate them. They crap all over the ledge. Did you know you can get sick from pigeon crap?"

He put the newspaper in the wastebasket and settled back in his chair. "I guess you're wondering what this is all about, so let me get right to the point. I spoke to the District Attorney's office about a week ago. They said they got a call from someone who thinks we need to reopen the investigations on the death of Danny Reedy, Quaid Perkins, Nadine Cavinet and Randy James. Now according to our records, all of the deaths, except for Danny Reedy, have been listed as accidental. His case is still open, but it's not in my jurisdiction. So I have been given the go-ahead to conduct another investigation on these cases. I'm gonna give it one more shot. That's where you come in. Have you ever heard of Stellar Productions?"

Mike nodded. "Sure, who hasn't? It's one of the largest recording companies in this part of the country."

"I thought you might have been familiar with it. Well, Jim Colby, the owner of the company is the one that contacted us. Either this is the worst scenario of coincidences I have ever seen in my career or I got some psychopath killer that is trying to bump off a whole band. That's what Jim thinks, too. He's real worried. Jim is afraid that something weird is going on and all of his people are real nervous. It's affecting his business.

I've interviewed everyone that was even close to the situation and I have come up empty-handed. You were picked to come here for two reasons. One, you come with good recommendations and second, I hear you're a hell of a musician."

Mike seemed surprised. He had no idea what playing the drums had to do with this case. "I know you're completely confused at this point, so I'm gonna let you read this file and I'll meet with you again after lunch." He stood up and handed a heavy folder to Mike, which was a signal for him to leave.

Mike put the folder under his arm and headed for the lounge. He stopped in the hall and bought a soda and bag of chips out of the vending machine. He sat down, put his feet on the coffee table and began to read. An hour later he pushed the papers across the desk and scratched his head. It was like a maze winding its way through Texas and Oklahoma with one common thread. Everyone that was dead had one thing in common. They all knew Carly Boone.

The Chester County Boys

Captain Gehring met him in the hallway. "So, Mike, what do you think? Except for Danny Reedy, do you think the other three who are dead were just unfortunate accidents or does it all seem like there might be a connection we just haven't been able to hit on."

Mike cleared his throat. "In my opinion, Sir, I think it is sure worth looking into. I'm not saying your force hasn't taken all the necessary steps to try and solve these cases, but I agree with you. It sure seems awfully coincidental."

"Exactly," Captain Gehring said, pointing his finger at Mike. "And that is where you come in. I need someone to infiltrate this band and see if they can find out what's going on. I don't have the manpower or the funds to put much into this kind of bullcrap, but if I don't do something, the D.A.'s office will be on my butt. I have all the details worked out with Jim Colby. You just need to show up at his ranch on Friday. Understand, this is all confidential and you are not to mention it to anyone. Study these files. It gives you some credibility in the music business. That's just in case someone gets nosey. You got any questions?"

"Yeah. Where can I get a good pair of boots?"

The next morning, Mike packed his duffle bag, sticking his badge and gun into the side pocket. He carefully covered his drums and loaded them into the back of his van. He smiled when he thought about what he was doing.

Mike Rotaglia grew up in a small town to optimistic parents that believed, in spite of everything, most people were decent. His father had been the sheriff of that town for over thirty years. Three of his brothers were in law enforcement. Mike never wanted to be a police officer. He wanted to be in the music business. His family never took his desire to be a drummer seriously. Before he really had an idea of how he was going to convince them of that fact, he was enrolled in the police academy. It was what his parents wanted.

After six years of patrolling the seamy side of life in Oklahoma City, and witnessing crimes that made him teeter on that fine line that separated police officer from avenger, he had enough. After chasing down a man who just raped and murdered a young girl, he sat on the man, his fist clenched wanting to smash his face and kill him. His gun in hand, he was only seconds away from pulling the trigger, when backup arrived.

Each time he held back his rage after someone spit in his face or physically attacked him, he became stronger. He was now more callous and less trusting of innocent faces. Sometimes it would take him days to shake it loose, making him question his desire to stay on the police force.

When his nerves got stretched to the limit, he would go into his garage, take the tarp off the shiny set of red drums and play them until his hands were sore and his ears could no longer hear the screams inside his head.

When he threatened to leave the police force, his brothers managed to pull enough strings to have him transferred to Tulsa and get him promoted to detective. Mike decided he could probably handle this position for a couple of years. It seemed like a gravy job compared to Oklahoma City. And now,

The Chester County Boys

maybe, just maybe, he might get a chance to play his music for someone who really appreciated it.

The next morning, Mike parked his van in the circle driveway of Jim Colby's ranch. Walking across the porch in his new boots, he tried to ignore the fact that they were killing his feet. The door chimes announced his presence and a small Spanish woman met him at the door.

"Studio," she kept saying, pointing to the low stucco building adjoining the main house.

He tipped his hat and grimaced as he walked the short distance to the studio. He pushed open the door and hobbled down a narrow hallway to another glass door. Merle was sitting in the studio with his feet on the desk and his hat pulled down over his eyes.

"Hello," Mike said, tapping on the glass.

Startled, Merle sat up and pushed the button on the desk that opened the door. "Come on in," he said. "Sorry, I just dozed off for a few minutes. I wasn't expecting anyone. Can I help you?"

"I'm looking for Jim Colby. Do you know if he is around anywhere?"

"He'll be back in about an hour. Have a seat. Unless you're in a hurry and then you'll just have to come back later."

"Naw, I can wait." Mike sat on the edge of the desk. His eyes scanned the room. "Man, this is top-notch equipment. I haven't seen a sound board that big in a long time."

"Yup, it's a nice one. Sure makes our band sound good. Are you a musician?"

Mike nodded. "Yeah, I play the drums." It sounded so good when he said it. "My name is Mike Rotaglia. You must be one of the Chester County Boys."

Merle smiled. "Sorry, I should have introduced myself. I'm Merle Hurley."

They made small talk for a few minutes before Merle got up and stretched. "I'll tell you something, Mike, all this sitting around is boring as hell. I didn't mind the tour, but making this demo is not my style at all. You play a few bars, and then you stop. Then you do it all over again. Some days we never even get through a whole song. I'm thinking Jim is just stalling and trying to keep us here until Carly settles down. She is a nervous wreck right now. But I can't say that I blame her. We sure have had some really bad luck," Merle yawned. "You know, when I was back in Lubbock, I'd sleep most of the day and play music at night. It sure was a much simpler life than I got now. I'm getting too old for this stuff. Yeah, I used to sleep till around two or three and then I'd pick up Quaid and we'd go somewhere and get a big, rare steak and a couple of beers. We played four sets a night. If it wouldn't be for my brother and Carly, I'd high tail it out of here right now. I bought a little cabin up at Dundee Lake. I can't wait to get up there and do some fishing. You like to fish, Mike?" He didn't give Mike a chance to answer. "Yeah, I sure miss old Quaid. He was like a brother to me. He didn't have the sense of a three-legged turtle trying to cross a six lane highway in rush hour, but he wouldn't hurt a fly. I sure can't believe he died in a swimming pool. Quaid was a real good swimmer. When we were kids, we used to swim in a quarry. I guess hitting his head was what made him drown. Poor old Quaid."

"I heard about that. That was a real misfortune," Mike said.

"Yeah, we had a lot of tragedy lately. First, it was Quaid. Then we found out someone killed that fella that Carly

The Chester County Boys

knew. Now, a couple weeks ago Randy and Nadine died in a fire. It just doesn't seem right. Carly is still stunned about what happened and so is Cletus. I was surprised Cletus took it so hard. Cletus never got along too well with Randy and he couldn't stand being in the same room with Nadine."

Merle didn't know it, but in the past fifteen minutes he provided Mike with a wealth of information.

"Hey, I'm sorry I've been bending your ear. I just haven't really had anyone to talk to. Seems like no matter what subject you bring up around here gets someone upset."

When Jim Colby arrived, he held the door open for Carly and then followed her into the studio. Jim had convinced Carly that now would be a good time to start on her album. It would help keep her mind off the latest mishaps.

Carly wasn't at all what Mike had expected. She was tiny, weighing maybe only a hundred pounds or so. She had ash blonde hair and dark eyes. "What are you staring at?" she said. "Do I have food on my face?"

"No, no. I'm sorry. I just pictured you differently in my mind," Mike exclaimed in an embarrassed voice.

"Well, sorry to disappoint you," she replied. She picked up her headphones and headed for the recording booth.

Cletus and Jack were now seated in the studio. Cletus bent over and whispered to Merle, "Who is that guy?"

"New drummer," Merle replied.

"Now who gave Jim permission to hire a drummer? He didn't say anything to us. This is still our band, right? I don't think we need a drummer."

Merle pointed to a chair. "Cletus sit down and shut up."

The room was quiet as Carly stepped up to the mic. She cupped her hands over her ears and began to sing a haunting song.

I didn't get a chance to tell you good-bye. You left while I was sleeping.

Now you're gone, and I'm alone, with memories not worth keeping.

I wanted to say I love you, but there is so much anger in my heart.

I wanted to say I'm sorry, let's make a brand new start. Is it too late now? Are you gone forever...

Mike leaned against the wall and watched her. She seemed out of place, like a sad little girl, but her voice was like velvet. He wondered how long it would take him to get through that tough outer shell that protected her.

After the session, Mike waited around until everyone had left except Jim. "I think maybe you and I need to talk," Mike said.

Jim looked around the room. He seemed nervous. "Not here. Let's take a walk."

They walked out onto the patio and sat down on the chairs by the pool. "Okay," Jim said. "I guess you know this isn't going to be easy. I'm not sure what is going on. I'm hoping all of these things were really just accidents, but I have to be sure."

"I understand," Mike said. "I have to go into town and find a place to stay and then I'll be ready to start my investigation."

"I have a better idea," Jim said as he pointed to the small brick building on the other side of the pool. "That's a guest house. It's real nice inside. You can stay there and you're welcome to eat in the house."

The Chester County Boys

"Are you sure?" Mike asked. "You have a lot of people out here already."

"Hell, that's a fact. When I told Carly she could stay out here, I didn't expect the boys to come with her. They just drove up in that old bus and unloaded their crap in my house like they were invited guests."

"Why don't you tell them to leave?" Mike asked.

"Right now, with all the craziness going on, I want to make sure what they are up to. I got a big investment and knowing them, they could screw it up in a heartbeat. I could just see Cletus giving interviews to anyone who would listen to him. In a few weeks, I'd be bankrupt. Besides, Carly seems to like having Merle around."

"Okay, now, Jim, tell me what you know for sure."

Jim was eager to give Mike as much information as he could. Mike got the impression from the way he talked that Jim and Carly were a couple. He made several inferences to Carly that surprised Mike. He mentioned that when the tour was over, he planned on taking her away on a vacation.

Mike agreed to stay in the guest house, saying it would be easier to get the investigation of the immediate people out of the way first. He did not tell Jim that it would include investigating him.

CHAPTER TWENTY-FOUR

Cletus was restless, again. He wanted to get back on the road. They had a show to do in Branson, Missouri and then on to Nashville. Jim had postponed both of the dates until further notice.

Cletus was tired of looking over his shoulder wondering if this would be the day that Jack would decide to bump him off or the cops would show up with a warrant for his arrest. He wondered how long it would be before they would be back on the road. At least when he was on tour he wouldn't have to spend most of his day with Jack. And then there was that new guy, Mike. He always seemed to be asking questions.

Lately Carly had warmed up to Mike and she seemed to enjoy having him around. Cletus was still angry that Jim had hired him without even consulting him. He felt like they were no longer the Chester County Boys, but just a backup group for Carly Boone. But, at least his face would be on the back of the new CD cover. Jim was also putting together a TV spot. So he shouldn't complain. He was getting closer and closer to Nashville.

Cletus wandered into the studio and sat down. He picked up his guitar and played a few runs, strumming out the melody to the last song on the CD. He turned to Jack who was sitting at the keyboard waiting for the rest of the group to arrive. "I'm going up to Merle's place this weekend to do some fishing, I was wondering if you would like to come with me? We can take the boat out on the lake and catch us a couple of big bass. Man, nothing tastes better than fresh, caught fish."

"Don't like boats, never been fishing and don't eat fish, so there ain't no use in me going," Jack replied without looking up.

"Well, I'll take a couple of steaks along, too. We can drink some cold beer and just relax for a day."

"Why are you asking me to go with you, Cletus? You and I aren't exactly good buddies. You wouldn't be thinking about doing something stupid, would you?"

Cletus laughed nervously. "Well, the truth of the matter is, I really hate your guts, but I think it may be a good idea for us to have a talk, you know at least be civil to each other. I thought it may give us time to do a little straight talking. That is, just in case, the police are still poking around. That's why I asked you to go."

Jack snickered. "That doesn't make much sense at this point, but I do have a few things I'd like to talk to you about. Yeah, it's really not a good idea to do too much talking around here. I'll go with you. Hey, I might even try my hand at fishing, but don't forget the steaks."

Whatever Cletus was planning would pale in comparison to the plan that Jack was now hatching in his head. Beer, lake, boat. Sounded like a winning combination to him.

On Saturday morning, Cletus pulled his Cadillac to the curb and honked the horn. He looked at his watch and drummed on the steering wheel. It was already six a.m. and he told Merle he would be up at the cabin by ten. He honked again and Jack stuck his head out of the door. "Hold your horses. I'll be there in a minute." Jack pushed the rest of his things into the duffel bags and headed for the door. Cletus honked again.

Once on the highway, Cletus became king of the road. Pushing the Cadillac up to eighty miles an hour, he swerved in and out of traffic. "Feel how smooth she rides, Jack. You sure don't get this out of a foreign car. Man, I love this automobile." He reached down with his right hand and pulled up his pant leg.

"Look here, Jack. Look at these, genuine rattlesnake boots. The best you can buy. Cost me eight-hundred dollars."

"You see, Cletus, this is what I mean. You are just beginning to taste the wealth. We can have it all if you keep your story straight and clam up about it. Hell, you'll be able to buy ten pair of them boots and a new Cadillac every year."

"What about you, Jack? What are you saving your money for? I never see you spending much. Hell, you don't even have a car."

"Don't worry about me. I got big plans for my money."

Two hours later, Cletus pulled up in front of Merle's cabin. He got out of the car and stood looking at the house. "Holy moley! Look at this place. This ain't no cabin, damn, this is nice, real nice." He let out a low whistle as he walked up the stone front steps to the entrance of the log house.

Once inside, Cletus dropped his fishing gear in the middle of the floor and yelled for Merle. He came around the corner of the kitchen drying his hands on a dishtowel. "Welcome to my new home," he said grinning. "First time in my life I ever owned a piece of real estate and I'm pretty proud of it. Course, I need to buy a few more things, but right now I got the basics: beds, refrigerator full of beer, a big television and a microwave.

"Come here, guys. I got something to show you." Merle opened the back door and stepped out on to the porch. "Now

The Chester County Boys

look at this, Cletus, I got a lake right in my back yard. I got a fishing boat down at the dock and a whole mess of bait. What do you think, little brother?"

"Nice. What's this lake called?"

"I named it Carly Lake."

"Wait just one minute. You mean you own the lake too? Where in hell did you get the money to buy this place? This is a prime piece of real estate."

"When we were in Lubbock I used to take Quaid over to the bank every payday to cash his check and it seems like he got friendly with a teller named Katherine. She convinced Quaid to let her invest some of his money. Well, Katherine did a real good job. After Quaid died, she sent me all the stock certificates. I was down as the beneficiary. I gave some of the money to Katherine and bought this place with the rest of it."

Cletus grumbled. "You could have given some of it to me instead of her. Hell, Merle, I'm your kin. You know I could have used the money. Anyway, one of these days I'm gonna have a big house in Nashville. How about you, Jack? Where you gonna live after the tour?"

Jack shrugged. "Don't know and don't care. I'm gonna look around," he said, taking a beer from the refrigerator.

Cletus watched him as he walked out the back door towards the lake. He jumped when Merle walked up behind him. "What's the matter with you, Cletus?" Merle asked. "You're as jumpy as a cat on hot coals. You got something on your mind I should know about?"

"Naw, just tired, I guess. You know, tired of studio work. I just need to get out on that lake and relax."

Jack lit a cigarette and leaned against a tree on the water's edge. He was angry. If he would have known Quaid had all that money he could have figured out some way to get it away from him. Instead, as usual, he got nothing. Maybe he would burn the house down before he left. It would serve Merle right.

Merle took the steaks off of the grill and opened a can of beans. He poured cold beer into glasses and announced that dinner was ready. "Now, this is real nice," he said. "It's good to be together again. Just like when we were in Lubbock. Course, I still miss Quaid and Randy."

He took a big bite of his steak. "Poor, old Quaid. He never did anybody any harm. I know Randy was a pain sometimes, but he was young. Yeah, I sure wish they were here."

Jack threw his fork on the table. "I'm not hungry. I'm gonna take a walk." He was tired of hearing about Quaid and Randy. Maybe he would burn the house down and make sure Merle was in it. He picked up a rock and tossed it into the lake and watched as it splashed and sunk into the dark water.

He hated water. He remembered when he was a kid and had to go to camp. The other kids made fun of him and pushed him in the pool. Choking and sputtering, he could see their laughing faces. He got even by putting garter snakes in their bunks. He joined the YMCA and learned to swim. He spent hours in the pool, swimming back and forth until his arms and legs felt like lead. He could probably jump in the lake right now and swim across to the other shore. He flicked his cigarette into the water and walked toward the cabin.

In the morning, Merle got up early and made coffee. He woke Cletus and told him to get up. "Let's go fishing. We got to catch us some breakfast."

The Chester County Boys

Cletus rolled out of his bunk and stretched. For a few minutes he forgot all about Jack and the trouble he was in. He pulled on his jeans and boots. "Okay, let's go. Those fish are waiting for us." It was just like old times; him and his big brother going fishing.

Merle and Cletus fished off the bank until the sun came up over the hills, turning the lake a rich shade of gold. The stringer in the water held four large bass and neither Merle nor Cletus were ready to quit. For the first time in months, they were having fun.

"Oh, look at this," Merle laughed. He poked Cletus in the ribs. Cletus turned to see Jack coming down the slope. He wore an oversized life jacket and wading boots. Cletus snickered. "What an ass."

"Okay, I'm ready," Jack said as he stooped down and began to crawl into the boat, pretending he was afraid of falling in. His fingers clutched the sides of the rail as he tried to steady himself.

Cletus waited until Jack was half way across before he stepped in behind him, causing the boat to sway from side to side.

"Stop it! Stop moving the damn boat until I get in!" Jack yelled, still holding on.

Cletus leapt onto the wooden seat and began to jump up and down. "How do you like this?" he said, laughing. "You can't swim a lick, can you, Jack?"

"I'm warning you, you little shit, if you knock me in the water, you're coming with me. I mean it. Now sit down!"

"Okay, okay, you two cut it out. We gonna fish or play games?" Merle said. "You two take the boat. I think I'll just fish off the bank."

Jack sat opposite Cletus and glared at him. Every once in a while, Cletus would lean over just enough to make the boat bob up and down. He now knew Jack's weakness and for once he felt like he might have the upper hand.

He pulled the cord on the small trolling motor and the boat skimmed across the water. Cletus navigated the boat around a bend and into a cove. "This looks like a good place to catch some big ones. You must be burning up in that life jacket. Why don't you take it off? You can sit on it." Jack pretended to reluctantly take off the jacket.

Reaching into the bait box, Cletus pulled out a large red worm. "You know how to bait?" he asked as he threaded the night crawler onto the hook.

Jack grimaced. "Give me one of them things." He put the worm on the hook and dropped the line into the water.

"That's not how you do it. You gotta get it further out in the water. You gotta flick your wrist," Cletus said. Standing up in the boat, he took the rod and cast it into the water. "See, that's how you do it."

Jack shifted his weight causing Cletus to sway back and forth as he tried to keep his balance. His rod swung up and down like an orchestra conductor's wand. Jack slid even closer to the edge of the boat and leaned into the water. Cletus tumbled forward grabbing Jack around the neck as the boat pitched sideways.

"Let go of me!" Jack yelled. "You got your finger in my nose. Let go!"

He pushed Cletus backward, sending him plummeting into the water with a resounding splash. Cletus disappeared below the surface for a moment and then bobbed up, sputtering and cursing at the same time. He grabbed onto the side of the boat, heaving his leg over the side, as he tried to get back in.

The Chester County Boys

Jack once again tried to push him in the water. They struggled, rolling from side to side. Their weight tipped the boat too far to the right. Jack jumped over the side as it began to sink, only to realize that he was standing in about three feet of water.

"You son of a bitch! You tried to drown me!" Cletus yelled, as he struggled to his feet, with streaks of mud running down his face.

"Oh, yeah," Jack replied. "And what the hell were you trying to do to me? Too bad you didn't pick a deeper spot. I would have held you under until your ugly face turned blue."

Cletus pulled his foot up out of the water. "Look at this," he said pointing to his bare foot. "My boot is stuck somewhere down in the mud. You owe me eight hundred dollars." He struggled across the short expanse of water and pulled himself onto the bank. "You stay away from me Jack Vance. I'm done playing games with you. One more of your sick tricks and I'm gonna tell Merle. I'm gonna tell him everything and you can bet your boots he'll be at the police station in a flash. And you better believe he is not going to blame me."

It was the wrong thing for Cletus to say. No one threatened Jack Vance.

By the time Merle reached the two men, they had most of the fishing gear on the shore and Cletus sat on the bank, pouring water out of his remaining boot. Jack's hair was plastered with mud and strings of green algae decorated his shoulders.

"What in the hell are you two doing? Where is my boat?"

CHAPTER TWENTY-FIVE

Carly laid her head back in the chair and closed her eyes. She felt the soft touch of the make-up brush wisp across her face. She still hadn't gotten used to having someone fuss over her and turn her into someone she hardly recognized in the mirror. She was never one to wear much make-up or style her hair. She now had a wardrobe of expensive clothes, hair extensions and veneers on her teeth. Jim had told her that appearance was everything.

The album was complete and ready to market. Jim had signed her up for several personal appearances on prime-time television shows. The radio stations were now playing her new single and it was climbing up the charts.

Jim had already started a campaign to promote her visit to the Grand Ole Opry after they finished in Branson. Carly was agitated that Jim had become her constant shadow. He stood behind her chair and watched as she was transformed into his little star. That was what he was given to calling her. Lately, he had assigned most of his other clients to his associates, telling them that he needed to concentrate on Carly's career. He was certain she would make his company a sizeable amount of money.

At first, Carly was grateful and flattered, but lately the attention that he was giving her began to make her feel uneasy. She felt a little like Eliza Doolittle, with Jim telling her how to stand, what to wear, and what to say on the television

The Chester County Boys

appearances. Jim's pats on the arm had now become lingering caresses around her shoulders and the once quick squeezes were now long hugs.

It was Merle who finally made Carly realize that she had to say something to Jim. Merle had told Carly that he was sure that Jim could make Carly a star, but he wondered at what price. Merle said that he knew Jim was totally awed by her and he was afraid that one day Jim would make his move. Merle was concerned and wanted Carly to have a talk with Jim before things went too far.

Merle was right, but Carly hadn't gotten up her nerve. She wanted to tell him that she was not ready for a relationship with him or anyone else. She was so grateful for everything he had done for her, but he was expecting way too much. She wondered how he would react. She had credibility now. Would he throw it all away and tear up her contract or would he get back to his business demeanor and laugh it all off? She wasn't sure.

Carly coughed as the hair spray wafted across her face. She waved her hand. "That's enough," she said and sat up in the chair. She smiled at Lonnie, her make-up man, to let him know she wasn't angry. She picked up a tissue and wiped her face.

"There is only one Dolly Parton, and I'm not her. I need to get some fresh air."

Jim followed her out the door. She was ready to scream at him to leave her alone, but it was Mike who saved her. He came around the corner just as Carly whirled around to face Jim.

"Wow, don't you look great," Mike said, letting out a low whistle.

Carly was relieved. She smiled and twirled around. "You like?"

"I like," he said laughing. "You got any plans for dinner tonight? I thought if you're not busy that you and I could go get a bite to eat somewhere."

Carly didn't hesitate for a minute. "No, no plans, dinner out sounds good. I have a television promo to do in about an hour and then I'm free for the rest of the evening. Why don't you go with me to the studio and then we can go to dinner?"

Jim stepped in between Carly and Mike. "I hate to be a wet blanket, but Carly's got an early morning show to do. She has to be up at six. I think she had better take a rain check."

Mike looked at his watch. "Don't worry, Dad, I'll have her home by eleven."

It was the wrong thing to say. Carly could see the small veins in the side of Jim's face twitch as he pulled his hands into a fist. He forced a limp smile. "I said, I don't think it's a good idea."

"We won't be late. See you later," Carly said, her knees almost caving. She had never disobeyed Jim's orders. She grabbed Mike's arm. "Let's go."

"What was that all about?" Mike asked as they drove toward Tulsa. "You're shaking."

"Just something I need to handle. Look, we don't really have to go out to dinner if you don't want to. I can catch a ride home from the studio."

"Why would you say something like that? Of course I want to take you to dinner. I have been meaning to ask you out for a couple of weeks now, but you always seem to be so busy and you seem to never take notice of me when we're together in the studio."

She smiled. "I've noticed."

They had dinner in a small Italian restaurant. Mike was a good listener. They made small talk for a while and Carly was

The Chester County Boys

embarrassed when a young girl came to their table and asked for her autograph. Mike laughed and told her to get used to being famous. This was just the beginning. She briefly told him a little about her past and then devoured her food. She didn't realize how hungry she was. "Gosh, that was good," she said. "I think I ate too much."

"Tell me," Mike asked, as she sat back in her chair, sipping on a glass of wine, "How did you ever get hooked up with the band? It just doesn't seem to fit."

"Every one asks me that same question. I guess when all this madness started I felt like I owed them, but now I just don't know. I love Merle to death. He takes care of me, but Cletus and Jack are only nice to me because I'm their meal ticket."

"And Jim, what is your relationship with him, are you two more than friends?" Mike asked.

"No, of course not. I don't even know if you can classify us as friends. I mean, I like him a lot, but after all, he is my boss. You know, he's kind of a father figure to me, but that is as far as it goes. Actually, lately he is starting to get a little too pushy. I really need to have a talk with him."

Mike smiled. "That's a relief. Now, tell me about Danny."

Carly stiffened. "Where did that come from? That's a part of my past I would just as soon forget about. I mean, who told you about Danny? He was just a guy I used to be with." Carly stood up and picked up her jacket. "I'm ready to go."

Mike took her hand. "I'm sorry, Carly. I didn't mean to upset you. I heard someone mention his name and I just wondered who he was. Let's just drop the subject."

They rode home in silence. When the car came to a stop in front of the ranch, Mike turned to Carly. "I had no business asking you about Danny. I won't bring it up again." He extended his hands. "Friends?"

She gave a limp smile. "Friends."

Mike and Carly began to see a lot more of each other. Mike was careful not to mention anything that would upset her. Jim had been called away on business which was a relief to both of them. Mike knew he wasn't concentrating on his investigation. Carly was occupying all his thoughts. She was so easy to be with.

They had just returned from dinner. Mike pulled his car up next to the house and got out. He opened the door for Carly. As she stood up, he pulled her into his arms and kissed her. She pulled away quickly. "Why did you do that?" she said, in a startled voice. "I thought you were my friend."

"I want to be more than your friend, Carly. I like you a lot and I just thought you felt the same way about me. We have been seeing a lot of each other and I thought it was time we moved the relationship forward."

"No! I'm just not ready for this." She ran up the steps and quickly went inside.

Mike stood there for a minute wondering what he had done to upset her so.

Carly didn't see Jim sitting in the darkened living room when she came in. She went straight to her room. She lay in her bed, tossing and turning. Why couldn't she learn to trust? Mike caught her off guard and it had taken her by surprise. The feelings inside of her were in turmoil when he was around. She really needed to talk to him. Putting on her robe, she quietly left the house and crossed the courtyard. She knocked softly on the guesthouse door. Mike opened the door. He was barefooted and

The Chester County Boys

wore only pajama bottoms. "I'm sorry I was so short with you tonight, Mike. I guess I'm still on the offensive about..."

Mike didn't let her finish her sentence. He put his finger over her lips. "No need to explain it to me, Carly. I guess I was just too anxious to learn everything about you. I care about you, Carly."

He slowly pulled her into his arms and kissed her. Leading her by the hand into the room, he dimmed the lights and flipped on the stereo. She didn't protest.

In the early light of morning, Carly opened her eyes to see Mike lying next to her. A stream of light filtered through the window landing on his back. He lay on his stomach with his hands wrapped around his pillow. She moved closer to him and put her leg over his. Carly drew circles in the small of his back until he began to stir. He turned over and grinned. She snuggled into his arms and listened to his rhythmic breathing. She felt safe. For the first time in years, she really felt safe.

"What's for breakfast? I'm starving," she whispered into his ear.

"I've got coffee and I can make you some Pop-Tarts. How does that sound?" Mike said.

Carly screwed up her nose. "Terrible. I want bacon and eggs and toast and orange juice."

"Okay," Mike said. "For that you need to get dressed. We'll have to go into town."

"So, if I choose Pop-Tarts I can stay in bed?"

"You bet," Mike replied as he got up.

"Then Pop-Tarts it is. I'd like mine well-done please." She scooted under the covers and waited for his return.

Later that morning, after Carly had left the guest house, Mike dressed and left for the studio. As he entered the front door, Mike was surprised to find that Jim had returned from his business trip. Jim pulled him aside. "Where have you been all morning? I've been looking everywhere for you. What the hell was that all about last night? Why did you ask Carly out?"

Mike wondered how Jim had found out about his date with Carly the previous evening. Regardless, he replied, "Look, Jim. How am I supposed to do my job, if I can't even talk to Carly? I know she must have some idea about what happened to all those people."

"So, that's all it was? You were just trying to get some information to help with the investigation?"

"Yeah, that's all it was." He hoped he had been convincing enough. Mike turned and walked away. What would Jim say if he knew Carly had spent the night with him? Things were getting complicated. He was on an assignment and knew that what he did last night was wrong. What he felt for Carly was not just a casual friendship or a one-night stand. He planned on seeing a lot more of her.

Over the next few days, Mike convinced Carly that it was better that Jim not know about their relationship. Carly understood. Cletus and Merle had both warned her that Jim was going to be hard to shake.

Carly seemed to feel the same way. It was fine with her. She decided that as soon as her contract was up, she was going to find a different manager. She wanted to make her own decisions about her future. She never knew that Jim was already hatching a plan of his own to take control of her completely.

The Chester County Boys

In the following days, Jim arranged personal appearances, television spots and rehearsals to keep Carly busy and away from Mike. He continued to postpone their appearance in Nashville, always giving some excuse that it would be best to wait just a little longer. He was irritable most of the time as he watched the relationship growing between Mike and Carly.

He wanted Mike out of her life and if he had to tell her the truth, he would. He also had his fill of the Chester County Boys and he wanted them gone, too. He was sick of Cletus constantly complaining and the brooding silence of Jack. With Carly constantly busy, the band had little to do but sit around the house. They were bored and ready to perform again. When Jim finally told them they were going back on the road, Cletus let out a whoop. "Hot damn, it's about time."

The two buses pulled out of the ranch two days later and made their first stop in Louisville, Kentucky. Jim had added the performance in Louisville as a surprise to everyone. The arena was packed. Carly had been added as a special guest. When the band and Carly took the stage, the audience applauded and stamped their feet. Cletus grinned from ear to ear as he stood as close to her as he could get. Several times Cletus jumped in front of Carly, raising his guitar in the air and doing his Elvis impersonation. The audience laughed.

Jim watched from the side of the stage, doing a slow burn. It was time to put an end to all of this nonsense.

After the show, Jim waited until the auditorium had emptied out and Carly had left the stage before he walked down the center aisle. "Good, I'm glad you're all here," Jim said.

Merle, Cletus and Jack wondered what he wanted now. Jim was famous for impromptu meetings and they were tired of always having to listen to his comments on their performances.

They assumed this was just another one of his stupid lectures. Cletus wondered why Carly and Mike were excluded from this meeting.

"Okay, let me get right to the point. The show tonight was lousy. You guys were way off key and Cletus, I don't know what the hell all that jumping around was supposed to be. You look like someone just gave you a hot foot. I am not going to Nashville or anywhere else and having you guys make a fool out of me. I've made a decision. I'll pay you for the rest of the tour and you'll get your share of the royalties from the CD, but as of tonight we are through."

For a moment there was silence. Cletus' jaw dropped open. Jim just stood there with his arms across his chest. "Well, any questions?"

Cletus broke the silence. "What in hell are you talking about? You can't do this. We got a contract. Tell him, Merle. We got a contract." He jumped up from the stool where he was sitting and faced Jim. "You better start laughing so I know you're kidding or I just might punch you right in the mouth."

"I'm not kidding, so take your best shot. This is it. You forgot to read the fine print, Cletus. I'm the one in charge and what I say goes. I am through with you. You can stay on the bus for the next few nights, but I want you all out of here by Sunday." He turned and left.

Merle slapped his knees. "Well, that's it for me. I guess I'm going fishing sooner than I thought. Anyone coming with me?"

"What do you mean, fishing? You're telling me you ain't mad as hell about what just happened? We're supposed to be standing on the stage of the Grand Ole Opry in just two days. Now that bastard just blew us out of the water. Do you think I have put up with his crap for almost a year to let him treat me

The Chester County Boys

like a bag of dirt? I ain't gonna be thrown off the bus like a bag of trash," Cletus yelled.

"Can't say I'm not sorry for you and Jack, but as for me, hell, I was ready to hang it up weeks ago. I'm too old for this nonsense. You do what you want, but I'm getting my stuff together and heading for the lake." Merle patted Cletus on the shoulder as he passed him and left the stage.

"What about you, Jack? You haven't said a word," Cletus said.

"What should we do about Jim?"

"I say we kill him," Jack said, clenching his fists.

"What? Are you nuts? We can't kill him. Maybe we can have someone kidnap him, you know, just until the show is over."

Jack shook his head. "That's no good. That would just mean more people in on our plan. We don't even trust each other. He could have an accident. The brakes on his car could fail or maybe he'll get food poisoning."

Cletus began pacing back and forth. "Be our luck, if he died they would stop the tour. No, I think we need to go to Carly and tell her what Jim is planning on doing and beg her to talk to Jim. Hell, I'm not proud. I'll beg. Jim likes her. She may be able to change his mind."

"And then what?" Jack asked. "What will we do if she can't talk him into it?"

"We'll kill him," Cletus mumbled.

CHAPTER TWENTY-SIX

Carly sat at the small table in her dressing room after the show in Kentucky. It was one of the better dressing rooms, since most were not much bigger than a closet. She was annoyed that Jim had arranged the performance in Louisville without her knowledge. She had no idea what he planned on doing next or that he had already fired the band. There was a light knock on the door.

"It's me," Mike said, peeking his head inside. He kissed her on the cheek and produced three red roses from behind his back.

Carly smiled. She was glad to see him. "I'll be ready in a minute. Thanks for the roses." She began lathering her face with cream to remove the layer of make-up. She winked at him as she wiped her face with a cloth.

They were now spending almost every day together. Mike helped her rehearse her songs and memorize her monologues. They ate together and spent the evenings watching television with Carly usually curled up in Mike's arms. She had learned to trust him, which was a new experience for her. He made no demands on her and for that she was grateful. It all seemed so natural, but sometimes the feelings inside her scared

The Chester County Boys

her. She knew she was falling in love with him and that was a big chance for her to take.

Mike sat quietly watching her in the mirror. When he left her last night, he decided it was time to tell her the truth. He was in love with her and he knew if he didn't tell her soon, it would be all over. Maybe it was too late already. How was she going to react when he told her that he was an under-cover detective? Would she slap his face or cry? He had no idea what she would do.

Carly was good at covering up her feelings most of the time. He tried to imagine how he would feel if the situation was reversed. Would he feel completely betrayed or maybe at least let her explain? His mouth was dry. As he reached for the bottle of water on the dressing table, she grabbed his hand and ran it down her cheek. This was going to be tough and he knew it. He had been summoned back to Tulsa and he needed to clear he air before he left.

"Carly, I have something I need to tell you. I want you to let me finish before you say anything," he said nervously.

She turned in the chair to face him. Was she ready to hear the words from him? Was he going to say he loved her? "Not now, Mike. Let me change my clothes and we can go somewhere quiet and talk."

He nodded. "Okay, I'll wait outside."

A few minutes later, Carly bounded down the steps. She kissed him on the cheek. "Where we going?" she asked as she got into his car.

"Let's just sit here for a few minutes." He ran his hand back and forth across the steering wheel as he began telling her a little bit about his background. He could see the puzzled look on her face, but she didn't interrupt him. When he finally got to the part about joining the police force and then making detective, her back stiffened and she opened her mouth to speak. Then she changed her mind.

"I could get in a lot of trouble for what I am about to tell you, but right now I don't care. My only concern is for you." He told her that Jim was worried that there may be someone in the organization that knew more than they were saying about the series of events leading to all the recent deaths and the police department in Tulsa was not really satisfied with the outcome of the case regarding Danny Reedy. So Mike was sent to find out if anything in the investigation had been overlooked. He never expected to fall in love on the way. He reached for her hands, but she pulled back.

Mike had said the words. He said he loved her. All of her life she had waited for someone to say they loved her and mean it. She never expected it to be someone that she now could not trust anymore.

"I can't expect for you to take this all in at once, but I promise you, I never meant to hurt you. You have become such an important part of my life, Carly. I really mean it when I say I love you," Mike said.

"So all the time we have spent together was just part of your job. Is that what you're telling me?" she asked.

"No, not at all. I was just supposed to find out if you or anyone else could recall something that might have slipped your minds about the accidents. Carly, I knew right away that you were not involved."

Carly moved closer to the car door. "Oh, please. How many entries about me do you have in your little book? I want you to leave right now." She reached for the handle of the door.

The Chester County Boys

"Listen to me, Carly. I don't know what else I can say or how I can convince you that it's true. I have to go back to Tulsa tomorrow, but I couldn't leave without talking to you first."

"I really can't believe this. You mean Jim has known all along who you were? I can't believe he has done this to me. You are two of a kind. I seem to be getter dumber rather than smarter each year. What a fool I've been." She opened the door and got out. She turned and headed across the parking lot toward the buses.

Mike rolled down the window and called after her. "Please, Carly. Think about it for a little while. I love you and I'm not going to give up this easy."

She stopped for just a moment. She really wanted to cry, but so many heartbreaks had left her without tears. Once again, love had grabbed her by the throat. She hated him and she hated Jim Colby. She needed to talk to Merle. He was the only one that could comfort her now.

Carly opened the bus door and stepped inside. Cletus and Jack sat at the small table, a bottle of whiskey and two glasses sat in front of them. "Where's Merle?" Carly asked. "I need to talk to him."

"He's gone," Cletus answered.

"Gone! What do you mean gone? Gone where?"

"He went into town to get some supplies. He'll be back later. Damn fool is getting ready to go back to his cabin. Jim Colby, that bastard, let us go tonight. He fired us. Can you believe it? I'm sure glad you're here, Carly. Jack and I need to talk to you."

"Not now, Cletus." Carly rubbed her forehead. "Just try to work this one out for yourself. I want to be alone for a while."

Cletus stood up and blocked the aisle. "Listen, Carly. I know I'm really a pain in the ass, but this is really important. You know that I have been looking forward to playing in Nashville since as long as I can remember. Now here we are, just a little over a day away and that ass let us go. I'm as low right now as I've ever been in my life. Please, Carly, won't you talk to him for us? You been looking out for us all this time, can't you just help us out one more time?"

"Okay, I'll talk to him, but right now just leave me alone." She bounded down the steps and ran across the parking lot to her own bus.

Carly lay down on the bed and buried her face in the pillow. She tossed and turned in her bed for over an hour. Sitting up, she wrapped the blanket around her and went outside. She sat on the steps of the bus with a box of tissues until she saw the headlights of a truck pulling into the parking lot. Carly stood up as Merle got out of the truck carrying two large bags.

"What in the world are you doing out here this late, darlin? You should be getting some sleep. Tomorrow is your big day," Merle said.

"I need to talk to you," Carly said, her voice cracking.

Merle set the bags in the back of the truck and put his arm around her. "Let's go inside."

In between sobs and blowing her nose, Carly told Merle about Mike. "I was such a fool. I should have known what I had with Mike was too good to be true. What am I going to do now?"

"You might want to give yourself a little time and really think about what happened. I have a feeling Mike might have been telling you the truth."

The Chester County Boys

"Now, Cletus tells me that Jim let you guys go. I just don't understand what is going on around here. I need you to help me make it through the next couple of days, Merle. I have to get my emotions under control and I have to go have a talk with Jim while I still have the nerve."

"Darlin, I'll stay as long as you need me. You be careful, Carly. Jim has a way of twisting things around to make himself look good. Do you want me to go with you?"

"Thanks, but I need to handle this one myself."

Merle stood up and walked Carly to the door of the bus. "Good luck. If he gives you any trouble you just let me know." Merle hugged her and watched as she headed toward the motel across the parking lot.

She knocked softly on the door of room number seven. Jim opened the door. "I need to talk to you, Jim. I know it's really late."

Jim grinned. "For you, Carly, I'll always have time. What's on your mind? Have you been crying?"

"I want you to explain your actions to me, Jim. I want you to tell me why you had me investigated by the police and why you kept Mike's identity a secret from me if I wasn't a suspect?"

Jim was startled. He couldn't believe that Mike had revealed himself to her. He had to find the right answer to this question. He slowly walked around the room. "As far as my part in this situation is concerned, I was only trying to protect you. You were definitely not under suspicion by me or anyone else. I just thought maybe there was someone in the organization that could recall something that would help convince you that all of the deaths were indeed accidents. It was only a precaution on my part. I had no idea that Mike would carry it as far as he did. It was only for you, Carly."

"But why, Jim? I can't believe you did this to the boys and me. I trusted you Jim."

Jim felt the panic starting to overtake him. He couldn't let Carly alienate herself from him. He cared too much about her and a lot was at stake with his company because of her. He knelt down in front of her chair and took her hands. "Carly, you have got to believe me. I am as shocked as you are that Mike took it upon himself to investigate you. We had an agreement from the beginning that you were definitely not a suspect. I knew how upset you were about everything that had happened and I thought maybe once and for all I could ease your mind."

"Oh, please, do you really expect me to believe that? Well, as soon as we get done with the performance tomorrow night, I am out of here. As I recall, I had a one-year contract and by rights it is already over. Find yourself someone even dumber than me, if that's possible."

Jim put his hands up. "Okay, okay. I know you're upset. Let's just get through tomorrow night and then maybe we can talk about this again."

Carly rolled her eyes. She couldn't believe what she was hearing. He just didn't get it. "By the way, I understand you fired the boys. Well, if you want me on that stage tomorrow, you better make sure the Chester County Boys are there too."

Jim's eyes narrowed, he gave a wry grin. "Please tell me you're not threatening me? I'll let them on stage if you agree to go back to Tulsa with me after the show. It will be just you and me alone at the ranch. I know if we spend some time alone, you'll see things my way."

The Chester County Boys

Carly hesitated. "Sure, why not. What have I got to lose?" she said, pretending that she had given in to him.

Jim smiled. "That's my girl." He bent down to kiss her. She turned her head, the kiss landing on her ear. "You don't worry about a thing. The buses will be ready to leave in about an hour. I'll see you tomorrow in Nashville. I've already sent the rest of the crew on ahead of us. I wanted you to have plenty of time alone, so you would be ready for your big night."

He had no intention of letting the Chester County Boys perform. It was only Carly's bus that would be pulling out. They would assume that she had not convinced him to let them perform. When Carly got to Nashville, he would call and tell her that they had changed their minds about the show and decided not to come.

He put his arm on her shoulder. "Now you just go back to your bus and get some rest. Tomorrow, I want you to have the engineers run through the rehearsal and sound check with you. I have some business to take care of, but I'll be there in plenty of time for the show." Once again he bent down to kiss her, but Carly slipped under his arm and out the door.

Carly walked across the dimly lit parking lot. She opened the door of the bus. "Merle, Jack, Cletus, come on. Pack your stuff. You guys can ride with me. Leave the lights on in your bus and hurry. We're going to Nashville."

Cletus let out a war whoop that resounded through the night air. It took them just a few minutes to get their stuff together and change buses. Carly instructed the driver that it was time to leave. She was not in the mood to go into detail about what had happened with Jim. All she knew was Jim had given in to her too easy. She was sure he was not going to keep his promise to let them perform. It was time to let him know that two could play his game. After tomorrow night she would be through with the entire music business.

Jim was on the telephone when he heard the droning of the bus motor. He pulled back the blinds and watched as Carly's bus pulled out onto Highway Sixty-Five, heading toward Nashville. He finished his conversation and hung up the phone. He grinned, thinking about the band still sitting on the bus in the parking lot not even aware that Carly was gone. He picked up the phone again. "Yes, I need a cab to pick me up in about ten minutes. I'm going to the airport."

As the bus rolled down the highway, Carly stared out the window.

Merle sat down next to her and took her hand. "You okay, darling? You look awfully sad tonight. You just pulled off a miracle for Cletus. How'd you do that?"

"I suppose you might say I sold my soul to the devil. But tomorrow night, I'm buying it back."

CHAPTER TWENTY-SEVEN

Saturday, Three a.m.

It was raining when the bus pulled into Nashville. Everyone was asleep except Cletus. He was too excited. Pouring himself a second glass of bourbon, he walked to the front of the bus and sat down next to the driver. He bent his head down and peered out the windshield in between the swish of the wiper blades. "So, this is it. Nashville, Tennessee, home of the Grand Ole Opry," he said.

The driver looked at him and smiled. "Yep, this is it. I can park in the back lot of the Opry building. There is a garage that most of the stars use so that they don't get bothered by fans or do you want me to park in the side lot?"

"Pull into the garage. Yeah, that would be great. I don't want anybody bothering us right now. We need to get some rest." Cletus leaned back in the seat and sipped his drink. He felt like a star.

Once the bus was parked inside the garage, the driver got out. "Well, good luck. I got to pick up another bus to drive back to Louisville." He took his canvas bag from behind the seat and left.

Cletus made himself another drink and got off the bus. He wanted to see if any others stars were here. The garage was empty. Looking around he saw a circle of bright light shining over a door across the empty expanse of concrete. He trotted across the garage until he came to the door.

Cletus turned the knob and looked inside. It was a plush lounge with couches and chairs facing a large television monitor. There was a bar with crystal glasses lined across it. He gave a low whistle. "Well, well, first-class star treatment."

Wandering around, he opened another door that led to a row of dressing rooms. Cletus wondered which one would be his. His thoughts were interrupted by a man's voice, which startled him. "Can I ask what you're doing here?" the man asked. He wore a security guard's uniform, his hand resting on his holstered gun.

Cletus tried to smile. He extended his hand. "I'm Cletus Hurley, one of the Chester County Boys. We're the headliners for the show tomorrow night. Well, actually I should say tonight, since it's almost morning," he said laughing nervously. "Just thought I'd come in and check out the accommodations. We got here early. Our bus is parked in the garage."

The guard put his hands on his hips. "You're supposed to come by the office and get security clearance before you start wondering around. You got any identification? I don't remember seeing your name on the roster."

"I'm glad you boys are on the ball. I wouldn't want just anybody wondering around in here. You want to come out to the bus with me and I'll get my license and union card?"

The guard followed Cletus and waited while Cletus boarded the bus and returned with two cards in his hand. "Hope this will do."

Cletus held his breath while the guard pulled out his flashlight. He looked at the cards and then at Cletus. "I guess you are okay. But be sure and come by the office around seven and check in. I suggest you get back on the bus and stay there."

"Sure enough. See you later," Cletus answered.

He waited until the man had disappeared around the corner before he went back to the lounge again. He went back through the door leading to the dressing rooms. At the end of the hallway, he turned the corner and there it was, the ramp leading to the stage.

His legs were weak as he stepped onto the carpet and slowly walked toward the velvet curtains hanging on brass rods. His eyes scanned the banks of lights and rope pulleys crisscrossing the ceiling. Cletus walked out on to the stage. His footsteps echoed across the walnut planks in the empty auditorium. He dropped to his knees and rubbed his hand across the worn spot in the wood. He could only imagine who had stood on this very same spot, Johnny Cash, Waylon and Willie, and of course, Elvis Presley. Now the name Cletus Hurley could be added. He went back to the bus and fell asleep.

Seven-Thirty a.m

Merle went to the security office and signed in the band. He then woke up Cletus and Jack. They went across the street to a Waffle House to have breakfast. Cletus asked the waitress if she wanted his autograph. She said no.

Nine a.m.

Carly was the last one up. She put on jeans and a blue shirt and made herself a cup of coffee. A young man knocked on the door and said that she was wanted in the theater. She met with the sound engineer and the lighting technician. They spent over two hours doing equipment checks. When they were finished, Carly walked around the grounds of the Opry House trying to clear her head.

Eleven a.m.

Cletus, Jack and Merle moved their clothing and instruments into the dressing room and took a tour of the auditorium.

Noon

Carly and the boys ran through their number in the lounge and then broke for lunch. In between bites of his roast beef sandwich, Cletus told them about his late night visit to the stage. "I'm telling you, it was the strangest feeling. It was as if Elvis was right there with me just giving me the green light to follow in his footsteps."

Jack shook his head. "You're nuts. Elvis never stepped foot on that stage. He performed in the old Opry building. He died before they built this building."

"Shut up, Jack. That's what you know. It's the same stage that was in the old building." Cletus threw his sandwich down and stomped out of the lounge.

Two p.m.

Carly took a short nap and then began going through her closet. She pulled out her favorite black jeans and shirt and took them to the wardrobe lady to be pressed. She made an appointment with the hairdresser and make-up artist for later that afternoon.

Three p.m.

    Jack and Merle got into an argument with Cletus about the outfit he had chosen to wear. They refused to let him wear a red-satin jumpsuit or his sequined boots on stage.
    Carly got a call from Jim. She told him that everything was just fine and running on schedule.

Four p.m.

    Cletus was dressed and pacing back and forth in his dressing room. He had changed into a white-satin outfit, draped in fringe. He made sure that he stayed away from Merle. He didn't want to have to change his clothes again. The hairdresser had touched up his hair with black dye and coiffed into an oiled pompadour.
    Some of the other performers were arriving and the garage was slowly filling with buses and limousines. Cletus was too nervous to even go out and talk to anyone. After all his years of performing, nothing came to close to what was happening tonight. He shivered just thinking about all the things that had happened in the last year to bring him to this point. It was all behind him, he just had to forget about it. From now on, he was on his way up. Some day, he would be walking out on this stage alone. He would be the headliner.

Six p.m.

A buffet of food was put out in the lounge for the performers. Cletus ran around introducing himself to everyone. Carly got a another call from Jim. His plane was running late, and he was still in Tulsa. He seemed pretty upset. With any luck, he still planned on being there for her performance at nine o'clock. She told him not to rush.

Seven p.m.

The stage producer gathered Carly and the boys together to make sure they were ready. She told Carly that there seemed to be some confusion. According to her schedule, Carly was supposed to sing with the house band. Carly said no, there must have been some mistake. She was singing with her band.
Cletus wanted to know if there was any chance of them doing an encore. The producer firmly replied, No! She reminded him that he should follow the program explicitly. She was agitated that she had to make changes in the schedule.

Eight p.m.

Carly took a shower and started getting dressed. Jack and Merle sat outside smoking. They both wore jeans and white shirts. Cletus rifled through his closet on the bus, looking for his sequined boots. He cursed and downed a glass of bourbon. Merle had hidden them. Sticking his head out of the trailer, he yelled, "Okay, where in the hell are they? What did you do with my boots?"

The Chester County Boys

Eight-Twenty p.m.

Carly and the boys entered the lounge and watched the opening of the show. They were on next. Cletus paced back and forth across the lounge.

Eight Forty-Five p.m.

The producer handed them their headsets and attached their microphones. She led them to the foot of the ramp.

Eight-Fifty-Five p.m.

Someone handed Carly a telephone. It was Jim. His plane had just landed and he was on his way to his limo. He should be there in about ten minutes. Carly let out a sigh of relief. She was sure they could be on stage before he arrived.

Eight Fifty-Seven p.m.

"Ladies and Gentlemen, this is their first time here in Nashville. Let's give a warm Opry welcome for Carly Boone and the Chester County Boys."

Carly turned to the boys. "Just to let you know, Jim doesn't know you guys are playing tonight. I agreed to go on alone. Don't worry. By the time he gets here, we should be done with our number. If we aren't, just keep playing."

Cletus just stood there with his mouth open and Jack cursed under his breath. Merle grinned at Carly and gave her a hug.

Nine p.m.

    Carly took a deep breath, put a smile on her face and walked on to the stage. She raised her hand and waved to the crowd. "Hi, I'm Carly Boone." She turned toward the band, "And these are the Chester County Boys." The audience applauded. Carly moved forward on the stage and stopped. She was supposed to sing her new single, the song she had been promoting throughout the tour. She turned to the band. "Play Crazy."

    Merle mouthed the word, "What?"

    She repeated, "Play Crazy."

    It was the first song she ever sang with the band, so it might as well be her last. She sang with all the emotion she could draw from her body. Her back-up singers, totally confused, just hummed along. Half-way through the number she glanced to the left side of the stage. Jim was there. He was clenching and unclenching his fist. She knew he was livid. She didn't care, but he wasn't alone. Standing along side him were two police officers.

    Cletus saw them at the same time. At first, he didn't know what to think. He tried to concentrate on the song, but his mind was racing. What were they doing here? Did Jim call them to have them bodily removed from the stage or was it something more? Whatever it was, he was now performing on the stage of the Grand Ole Opry. That was something that could never be taken away from him. There was no way he was going to be arrested tonight.

    Jack, sitting at the keyboard, had his back to the left side of the stage and had no idea what was going on. Cletus slowly moved further back, until he was even with the back-up singers.

As soon as the song ended, he slipped into the shadow of the lights. He could see Merle watching him. Cletus tipped his hat to his brother and exited to the right side of the curtain.

Nine-sixteen p.m.

The performance was over. Carly listened to the applause. She bowed and thanked the audience. She walked off the stage expecting Jim to scream at her. "How could she let the band play when he said absolutely not? Why did she change her song?" But he was quiet. He stepped aside as Carly passed him.

One of the officers stepped forward and stood in front of Jack. He hadn't seen the officers until it was too late. He had no where to go.

"Robert Bedermann, you are under arrest for murder and unlawful flight from a federal institution. You have the right to remain silent and anything you say…" He put Jack's arms behind his back and handcuffed him.

Carly touched the arm of the officer. "Who is Robert Bedermann? This man's name is Jack Vance." She was stunned.

"I'm sorry, Ma'am. I can't give you anymore information. I have orders to take this man into custody." Jack said nothing as he was led away.

Carly turned to Jim. "Do you have any idea what is going on?"

"No. They wouldn't give me any information. They were already here when I got here. This is one hell of a mess. What happened here tonight? I thought I told you not to let the band perform. Other than the fact that you totally disregarded my orders and let those idiots on the stage and changed the program, I have no idea what is going on. I have half a mind to cancel our trip to the ranch."

Carly looked at him as though he had lost his mind. "That's good, because it isn't going to happen anyway," Carly said in an annoyed voice. "Merle, where is Cletus? I didn't see him exit the stage."

Merle threw his hands up in the air. "I don't know. What in the hell is going on?"

Nine -Twenty p.m.

Cletus had seen everything from the right side of the stage. He stood obscured by the curtain watching as the officers took Jack away. He wondered why they handcuffed him. Surely Jim wasn't pressing charges. A tap on his shoulder, made Cletus jump. His back stiffened as he turned around. "You okay?" Cletus stood facing one of the stagehands.

"Uh, yeah. I just felt a little queasy. That's why I left the stage. What's going on over there?" Cletus asked, pointing to the commotion on the other side of the stage.

"Man, they just arrested your keyboard player for murder. You better get over there and see what's happening."

Cletus gulped. "Oh, that's probably just some kind of joke. We are always pulling pranks on each other. Say, can you get me out of here without me having to face all those reporters? I need to get to my bus. I really don't feel good."

The stagehand nodded toward a golf cart parked behind the stage. "Come on, I'll take you out the back way. Boy, you guys must have a great sense of humor. I wouldn't think a stunt like that would be so funny."

The Chester County Boys

Nine-Thirty Seven p.m.

    Cletus changed into a pair of jeans and a blue shirt. He threw his guitar over his shoulder and picked up his duffel bag. Looking both ways, he stepped off of the bus and headed for the street. He put his hand up and hailed a taxi.

Nine-Forty p.m.

    Cletus was out of Nashville, heading south on I-65.

Nine-Forty-Five p.m.

    Suddenly reporters and photographers surrounded Merle and Carly. Carly shielded her eyes from the flashing lights. There was a barrage of questions with everyone talking at once.
    Jim took Carly by the arm. "Come on, let's go. I chartered a plane. We'll talk about all this on the way home."
    He pulled her down the ramp and into the lounge with a parade of people behind them. Merle followed, pushing the door closed to prevent the crowd from descending on them again.
    Carly uncurled Jim's fingers "Let go of me. I'm not going anywhere with you. Our association ends right here."
    Jim's eyes flashed. "You come with me or you're going to be sorry. I'm going to sue you for everything you own!"
    "Do it! All I have is an extra pair of jeans. By the way, have you ever heard of sexual harassment?"
    Jim glared at her and grabbed her arm again. "Let's go!"
    Merle stepped forward. "Take your hands off of her right now." He pushed Jim against the wall.

"I'll see you in court, too," Jim yelled at Merle. Squeezing out of the door, Jim held up his hands to the reporters and forced a smile. "Now, if you just give me one question at a time, I'll try to answer you."

Carly sat down on the couch in the lounge. "There is no way I am going out there, Merle. When things calm down, we have to go by an ATM. I need to make a withdrawal."

"Let's go out the garage door. Maybe we can make a run for the bus. We need to get our stuff and get the hell out of here." Merle opened the door and once again was met with a crush of reporters. "Maybe we better sit tight for awhile. I wonder where Cletus is?"

Ten-Thirty-Five p.m..

Merle and Carly were finally able to get to the bus. "Looks like Cletus was already here. His stuff is gone," Merle said as he stuffed his shirts into his suitcase. "Let's get our things together and hit the road. I can't take any more of this excitement."

Eleven p.m.

Merle and Carly were in the back seat of a pickup truck belonging to one of the stagehands. They had no idea where they were going.

CHAPTER TWENTY-EIGHT

Merle and Carly rented rooms in a hotel on the outskirts of Nashville. They registered under fictitious names. The press was still looking for them. There were a lot of unanswered questions about Jack Vance. They decided it would be better to hide out for a few days.

Carly hired an attorney named Tom Fortess, and he managed to find out some of the details. It seems that when the skeletal remains of Danny Reedy were found there were strands of hair twined around his fingers. When the DNA in those strands was put into the police database, they matched those of one Robert Bedermann. His whereabouts were unknown. When Mike was doing his investigation at the ranch, he obtained hair samples from everyone. Jack Vance and Robert Bedermann was one and the same person. That was the clue that connected him to Danny's death.

Two days later, when Cletus had not yet surfaced, Merle was given a pass to see Jack. "Well, look what the rat drug in. What are you doing here?" Jack said. He sat down opposite Merle, putting his cuffed hands on the metal table in the visiting room.

"I got just one question for you, Jack, or whatever your name is. Why did you do it?"

"One reason, Merle, money. I figured if I could hang onto Carly's coat tails long enough, I could get enough money together to get out of here for good. I was planning on going to Europe or maybe South America. I bet you have a few more questions, don't you, Merle? We might as well get this over right now. I don't figure I'll be seeing you again."

"Why did you kill Danny? Did he come after you?"

"I didn't kill him. It was all your brother's idea. I just wanted to scare him, but Cletus talked Quaid into pushing Danny off the cliff."

"I don't know if I buy that, Jack. Cletus hates violence. The one thing I want to know for sure is if you killed Quaid?"

"No. He was all spooked after what happen to Danny and I think Cletus must have got him riled up. I don't know how he ended up in the pool."

"I guess you're gonna tell me you had nothing to do with Nadine and Randy's deaths either?" Merle asked.

"Nope, had nothing to do with that either. I tell you, Merle, I plan to beat this wrap. Even the one about me killing the guard is a trumped-up charge."

"You know what, Jack? I think you're full of bull crap. I'm not buying any of this."

"You can think what you want, Merle. I don't have any hard feelings against you. You were always fair to me. And I like Carly. But, I'll tell you one thing, when I get out of here I'm gonna find Cletus. He's gonna be real sorry he turned me in."

"Speaking of Cletus, do you know where he is? He hasn't surfaced since we were in Nashville."

"No, but if he knows what is good for him, he'll stay away from me." Jack stood up as the guard came into the room.

The Chester County Boys

"Don't kid yourself, Merle, it was Cletus. He probably made some kind of deal with the police to get himself off the hook. I'm gonna get him, Merle. That's for sure." He turned and left.

Jack knew that he was going to be extradited back to Tulsa the following morning. He had to make a plan. Sitting on the bunk in his jail cell, he poured himself a full glass of water and dropped in a bar of soap that he found on the sink into the glass.

Shaking it vigorously, he removed the bar and drank all of the soapy water. He shivered from the taste and laid down on his bunk. Half an hour later the stomach cramps began. He moaned and groaned in his cell, telling the guard that his stomach was killing him. He spent most of the night on the toilet.

The next morning, he was handcuffed and put in a patrol car for a trip to the airport. The jail guard told the two officers that Jack wasn't feeling good and had been up all night with diarrhea.

Once in the patrol car, Jack waited until they were over a mile away from the station. He laid his head back on the seat and pulled his legs up to his chest, letting out foul smelling farts. He begged the officers to stop and let him go to the bathroom. He said he could feel the diarrhea coming on. They were seasoned officers and knew every trick in the book, but neither one was looking forward to cleaning up a mess in their patrol car and the smell was starting to get to them.

Stopping at a service station, one of the officers went inside while the other escorted Jack to the bathroom. Jack leaned over, moaning, and walked in small steps. The officer took the handcuffs off of him and pushed him into the bathroom. He warned Jack not to try any funny business because he would be outside with his gun ready.

Jack continued his act as he wretched and groaned loud enough to be heard outside. Flushing the toilet several times, he stood behind the door. The officer waited until everything was quiet and he was sure Jack was finished.

With his hand on his gun, he knocked on the door. Jack did not answer. The officer knocked again. He then told Jack to open the door and come out. Jack did not answer. Becoming agitated, the officer, with his pistol in his hand, turned the handle and opened the door.

Jack grabbed him by the neck and pulled him inside. He shoved the officer against the wall and banged his head against the cold tile with all his strength. The officer slid down the wall, leaving a trail of blood behind him. Jack grabbed his gun and car keys and made a run for the patrol car.

Just as he reached the car, the second officer came out of the station with two cokes and a bag of chips. He dropped them to the ground and yelled at Jack to freeze. Jack swung the door open and dove inside. He headed toward the street as the officer fired off two rounds, one of them narrowly missing Jack's head.

Two blocks from the station, Jack pulled the car into a dark alley and got out. The police would probably think he was heading toward the highway by now. Taking off his blue prison shirt, he tossed it into the car. In his white tee shirt and jeans he loped down the alley, jumped a fence near a junkyard and disappeared. An APB was put out for him and the police covered the area. Jack was not found.

The Chester County Boys

Nashville was buzzing with the news of The Chester County Boys and Jack Vance. Carly and Merle watched the story unfold and saw their faces on every television station and in the newspaper. No sordid detail was left undone. Jack's picture was everywhere.

He was touted as a cold-blooded killer. Carly and Merle were as stunned as everyone to find out about Jack's record and the fact that he was involved in several killings. The tabloids picked up the story and Merle was portrayed as an over-the-hill guitar player. They called Cletus a midget Elvis wanna-be, who also seemed to have vanished. Carly was called the poor little waif who got caught up in the horrors of the music business run by a ruthless man named Jim Colby.

The police were curious as to why Cletus took off and questioned Merle several times about his whereabouts. Merle said he had no idea where he went. Knowing that he had time to get to the bus and get his stuff, Merle was sure Cletus was on the run.

On Tuesday, Carly found out that her single was number one on the Country Charts. Her song was being played on every Nashville station. For the first time in quite a while she and Merle had a good laugh. She wondered when she would hear from Jim. It didn't take long.

Carly's attorney called saying he had received a letter from Jim. Jim said he would not sue Carly for breach of contract if she would sign over all rights to the single and her CD. She also had to agree not to sue Jim for any reason. Carly said if a clause was added that stated if she resumed her singing career at any time, Jim would have absolutely no claim on her, she would sign it. Jim agreed and the papers were quickly finalized.

After four days confinement in their hotel rooms, Carly and Merle decided it was safe to venture out. The police wanted to question them again. "Well, we might as well go and get this over with. I don't know what else we can tell them," Carly said as she and Merle sat in the back of the taxi, both wearing dark glasses. "Since I got Jim off my back, this should be the last hurdle. Maybe they will let us leave this damn town."

"I hope so, darlin, I sure hope so," Merle replied.

Carly's lawyer was already at the station when they arrived. They jostled their way through the press photographers and ignored the questions from the reporters. Once inside, Carly walked up to the lead detective, "What do you want now?" she asked.

"I have some good news for you. You are free to leave town. Jack's case has been turned over to the FBI. There is nothing that connects you two to any of the deaths. A lot of the work was done by a Detective Michael Rotaglia. He was the one that broke the case. I just have one final question before you leave," the detective said. "Do you know where your brother is?"

Once again, the answer was no.

Merle and Carly left Nashville in less than an hour.

CHAPTER TWENTY-NINE

Merle sat in a lawn chair on the dock. His fishing pole, which had long since lost its bait, dangled in the water. He never tired of looking at the lake. In the morning when it was smooth as glass, he could see the reflection of his house and trees in the water, giving him an all new perspective. In the evening he would watch the large-mouth bass cut through the water chasing the green frogs that ventured away from the security of the shoreline. But, today, he had something else on his mind. He hoped he hadn't made a huge mistake. He would find out real soon.

Life had settled down in the last two weeks since Merle and Carly arrived at the cabin. Carly was amazed at how the fresh air affected her. She arose early, but by mid-afternoon she was ready for a nap. Merle's cooking had forced her to open the top button on her jeans when she sat down. She and Merle talked about what happened the last year and tried to make some sense of it.

Carly was still curious as to why Jack killed Danny, or how they even met. She had come to the conclusion that she would probably never know. She thought a lot about Mike. He had hurt her deeply, but Merle was still trying to convince her that it had never been his intention.

Carly awoke from her nap and stretched. It was another beautiful day. Shoving her feet into her tennis shoes, she rose from the couch and headed toward the porch. She was sure that Merle was probably fishing.

Sitting by the lake was where he spent most of his time. Trotting down the path, she stepped onto the dock, causing Merle to stir. "I'm sorry, Merle, I didn't mean to wake you." She sat down next to him.

"I wasn't asleep, Carly. I was just kind of day dreaming."

She hugged her knees. "About what?"

"Oh, just wondering why I bought such a big house. Maybe after all the craziness of this past year, I just went a little off the beam. It sure is out of character for me. You know me, Carly. I'm not a very deep person. Hell, I've always hung out on the fringe of life. I never really wanted to get involved in much of anything and I hate making decisions. That's why I only own two shirts; both of them are blue denim. All my socks are white and I always buy black, Ford trucks."

"What about your music, Merle, didn't that count for anything?"

"I guess when I was a kid, Cletus had me convinced that we were going to be big stars, but as the years went on, it was just a job."

Carly lay down on the dock and let the warm sun hit her face. "Okay, then what about the time you took care of me and what about Quaid? You took care of him all those years."

"I kind of messed up on both counts, didn't I? I should have never stopped looking for you and poor Quaid got himself done in because I made him go on the tour."

The Chester County Boys

Carly sat up. "Merle Hurley, I can't believe you. You have spent the last year trying to convince me that I wasn't responsible for all the crazy things that were happening and now listen to you. You would have never found me; I was lost in the system, and Quaid's death sure wasn't your fault. I still say if I hadn't started singing with the band none of this would have happened. Quaid, Nadine and Randy would still be alive. Even that crazy Danny wouldn't have got himself killed."

"You just can't let it go, can you, Carly? If it wouldn't have been you, maybe it would have been another singer or maybe Jack would have just got mad and killed us all. Hell, we didn't have to tag along with you when you left the Double L. If anything, we caused our own problems. Cletus could have come to me and told me what was going on from the beginning. But he was too hell-bent on going to Nashville. You can't change the past. Things happen that we have no control over and you can't spend the rest of your life trying to make them right. You just got to move on. Look at me, I'm moving on."

They sat in silence for a few minutes, with only the sound of the insects buzzing over their heads.

"So what are you going to do now?"

Merle pulled his line out of the water. "I'm doing it. As long as I got my health, I'm gonna stay right here. I got enough money to last me for the next twenty years or so and after that I'll be too damn old to care." He threw the line, now baited with a fresh worm, into the water. The red and white bobber dipped in an out of the lake. "What about you? You got any plans? Have you thought at all about Mike?"

"Yes. I really liked him. I wished things could have turned out differently for us. You know, Merle, I have felt so safe here the last two weeks that the thought of going back out into the world scares me to death. I have some money, too. I should be all right for a while. I can't believe I'm saying this, but the music business still interests me. I just need to go at it from a whole new approach."

"Well, darlin, you can stay here as long as you want. In a couple of months things will all settle down and then maybe you can find yourself a decent agent." Merle yanked on his line and pulled up another empty hook. "I guess these fish are getting too smart for me. I think I'll call it a day."

Carly stood up. "You know what? I haven't taken a swim in the lake yet. I think I'll do it right now."

"You go right ahead. I'll go up to the house and get you a towel."

Pulling her shirt over her head, Carly kicked off her shoes and removed her jeans. She dove head first into the water, almost losing her breath as she sunk below the surface. The water was freezing. She came up squealing.

Merle turned and yelled at her. "It's spring fed, Carly, the water never gets warm."

Carly treaded water for a few minutes and then swam out to the middle of the lake. Her body was beginning to get used to the temperature of the water, even though her feet felt numb. Swimming back, she circled the dock as she heard the sound of footsteps on the wooden planks.

"Here's your towel."

Carly raised her hand; she was face-to-face with Mike. He was bending down with the beach towel draped across his arm. Her eyes widened.

"What are you doing here!"

"I could say I was just in the neighborhood, but the truth is Merle invited to come visit for a couple of days."

The Chester County Boys

"Did he tell you I was here?" she asked.

"Yes, he did. That's why I came. I really need to talk to you," Mike answered.

He extended out his arm. "Do you want this towel?"

"Keep it." Carly swam away from the dock.

"I quit my job with the department, Carly," he called after her.

"Good for you," she scoffed.

"Are you coming out?" Mike asked.

"No. And don't ever talk to me again."

"Okay, then I'm coming in." Mike stood up, pulled his wallet and keys out of his pocket, and laid them on the dock. He took a few steps and jumped into the lake.

Carly turned her head as the water splashed her face. Mike surfaced like a clown shot from a cannon. "Holy, son of a …this water is freezing." Treading water, his teeth chattering, he asked, "Are you going to talk to me before some of my body parts start falling off?"

She didn't answer. She swam to the dock and quickly pulled herself up on the moss-covered steps. Grabbing the towel, she wrapped it around her shoulders and ran toward the cabin. She flung open the door and yelled, "Merle Hurley, I am so mad at you. Don't ever talk to me again!"

Merle was in the kitchen making corn bread and catfish. He shook his head. "Yep, something tells me I made a huge mistake."

An hour later dinner was ready. Mike had changed his clothes and was sitting by the fire drinking a cup of coffee. Carly hadn't come out of her bedroom. Merle tapped lightly on the door. "I got dinner ready; are you hungry?" There was no answer. "Okay, but you're missing a good meal."

Carly came into the dining room, her hands shoved in her back pockets. Mike and Merle both stopped eating and waited until she slowly pulled out her chair and sat down. "I'm hungry, but don't either of you talk to me." Carly put the catfish on her plate and filled a bowl with slaw. She picked up her fork and began to eat.

"Carly, can you pass the salt?" Merle asked.

Carly shoved the shaker across the table. Looking around, she reached for the catsup, but Mike picked it up. "I'm sorry, do you want this?"

"Yes," she answered.

"Are you talking to me?" he asked.

Mike complimented Merle on the dinner and told him how refreshing his swim was. Carly said nothing.

Merle went to the kitchen and returned with a pot of coffee and dessert. He poured a cup and handed it to Carly. "By the way, Mike, I want to thank you for fixing it so Carly and I could leave Nashville. That sure was nice of you. I got some questions and I wonder if you could maybe give me some answers?" he said, glancing at Carly.

Carly slowly stirred the cream into her coffee. As much as she wanted to leave the table, she knew that Merle was prodding Mike for her benefit. She wanted to know what he had to say. She pretended to be disinterested, concentrating on her chocolate pudding.

"I'd like to believe that Jack was just protecting Carly when he killed Danny, but I'm afraid he just wanted to keep Danny away from Carly for his own selfish reasons," Mike said.

"Jack had an agenda all his own. After being convicted for manslaughter and then killing a prison guard, he had to keep a low profile. He could get lost in the country music business with his altered appearance and still make money. I'm sorry, Carly, but you were his meal ticket. I'm also sorry that I had to be the one doing the investigation. I had no idea what I was getting into when I took the assignment. It wasn't my intention to hurt you," Mike said, staring at Carly.

She was silent.

"I guess Quaid, Nadine and Randy all got in the way. Jack was a real piece of work," Merle said. "I always thought he was kind of spooky, but I never thought he was capable of murder. Of course, Cletus is the only one that can give us the real story about how Jack was able to pull it all off, that is, if he ever surfaces again. I should have known that he was mixed up in all of this."

Mike sipped his coffee. "I don't think Cletus killed anyone. He just got caught up in all the hype. I think Jack had him convinced that everything would be okay after Danny died and then things just snowballed and Cletus was so deep in it, he couldn't get out. I think he was really scared of Jack and also he wanted to get to Nashville so badly, he just kept his mouth shut."

Merle stood up. "I sure hope you're right. You know, I'm really beat. Do you guys mind cleaning up? I'm gonna hit the sack." Merle gave a pretend yawn. "Good night, you two."

He winked at Mike and left the room.

Carly stacked the plates and carried them into the kitchen. She filled the sink with soapy water while Mike cleared the rest of the dishes. He put them on the counter. "Look, Carly, if I haven't a chance at all with you, tell me right now. I'll pack my clothes and leave in the morning. If you're just trying to punish me some more, I deserve it, but one of these days you're gonna have to talk to me. Which one is it?"

"If you would have asked me that question two weeks ago I really don't know what the answer would have been," she said softly. "I've done a lot of soul searching since then. I know that I would be lying if I said I didn't care about you, but I'd also be lying to you if I said what you did doesn't still bother me. Merle has convinced me that everyone deserves a second chance.

Mike drew her into his arms, her soapy hands landing on his neck. "I'm so sorry, Carly. I don't know how many times I can tell you that I really never meant to hurt you." She buried her face in his chest.

"Maybe we can start over. Take it slow this time and really get to know each other. In time you may learn to trust me again. I love you, Carly."

"Maybe that would be a good idea," she replied.

"What are your plans now?" Mike asked.

"I'm not real sure, but I have a few ideas that Merle and I have talked about. I think I want to stay out of the music business for a while. When I do get back into it, I want it to be on my terms. I would also like to take a trip to Massachusetts to see a friend of mine. Her name is LouJean Bailey. Knowing LouJean, I bet she is freaking out over all this stuff in the paper. Maybe you would like to go with me.

"Sounds good to me," Mike replied.

Merle found them asleep on the couch in the morning, their arms wrapped around each other. Carly shifted her position and opened her eyes. "Hi, Shine," she said grinning.

Merle slapped his knees. "Good morning. Am I forgiven, too?"

"Yes, you are. Thanks."

"Good, I'm leaving." He picked up his duffel bag sitting by the door. "I'm going to find Cletus before Jack finds him. You two take care of my house."

Carly sat up. "How do you even know where to look?"

"Bad musicians are like snakes in the sand. They leave a pretty good trail. Besides, I know my brother. He can't stay out of the limelight too long. I'll find someone who knows where he went."

"You're not going to hurt him, are you, Shine?" Carly asked.

"Nope, I'm just gonna kill him."

La Hoya, Mexico
Cantina Del Roho

Two musicians sit in the shadow of the stage in a sleazy, smoked-filled cantina. As the runway lights come on, a man in a large sombrero takes the stage and taps on the mike. "Senoritas and Senors, please welcome for your entertainment, Senor Cletus Hurley, star of the Chester County Boys and The Grand Ole Opry."

As the announcer passes Cletus on his way up to the stage, he says, "I expect a good show. By the way, Senor, I hired a new keyboard player today."

THE END

For more information on Marlene Mitchell
or synopses of Marlene's other awesome novels:

www.bearheadpublishing.com/marlene.html

Printed in the United States
135165LV00002B/6/P